Everyman, I will go with thee,
and be thy guide

THE EVERYMAN
LIBRARY

*The Everyman Library was founded by J. M. Dent
in 1906. He chose the name Everyman because he wanted
to make available the best books ever written in every
field to the greatest number of people at the cheapest possible
price. He began with Boswell's 'Life of Johnson';
his one-thousandth title was Aristotle's 'Metaphysics',
by which time sales exceeded forty million.*

*Today Everyman paperbacks remain true to
J. M. Dent's aims and high standards, with a wide range
of titles at affordable prices in editions which address
the needs of today's readers. Each new text is reset to give
a clear, elegant page and to incorporate the latest thinking
and scholarship. Each book carries the pilgrim logo,
the character in 'Everyman', a medieval morality play,
a proud link between Everyman
past and present.*

Gonzalo Torrente Ballester

THE KING AMAZ'D
A CHRONICLE
Crónica del rey pasmado

Translated and Edited by
COLIN SMITH

Consultant Editor for this Volume
MELVEENA MCKENDRICK
University of Cambridge

EVERYMAN
J. M. DENT · LONDON
CHARLES E. TUTTLE
VERMONT

Crónica del rey pasmado © Gonzalo
Torrente Ballester, 1989 and Editorial Planeta,
S.A., Barcelona, 1989

Introduction and other critical apparatus
© J. M. Dent 1996

First published in Everyman Paperbacks in 1996
in association with the Ministerio de Cultura, Spain

Translation © Colin Smith 1996

J. M. Dent
Orion Publishing Group
Orion House
5 Upper St Martin's Lane
London WC2H 9EA
and
Charles E. Tuttle Co. Inc.
28 South Main Street
Rutland, Vermont 05710, USA

Typeset in Sabon by CentraCet Ltd, Cambridge
Printed in Great Britain by
The Guernsey Press Co. Ltd, Guernsey, C. I.

British Library Cataloguing-in-Publication Data
is available upon request.

ISBN 0 460 87730 5

CONTENTS

NOTE ON THE AUTHOR
AND TRANSLATOR

GONZALO TORRENTE BALLESTER was born on 13 June 1910 in Ferrol, Galicia, north-west Spain, in the bookish family of a naval officer. He read history at university and worked in early days as a journalist and then as schoolmaster, from 1947 being much involved in the literary life of Madrid as anthologist, editor, and critic, and also as author of plays and novels which attracted little attention. He began to have success with the trilogy of novels (1957–62) about Galician life in the 1930s entitled *Los gozos y las sombras* (*Joys and Shadows*), followed by *Don Juan* (1963) and *Off-side* (1969). From 1966 to 1970 he had a post as visiting professor at Albany, USA, and there wrote much of his finest book, *La saga/fuga de J.B.*, published in 1972, a classic of (de)mythologizing and of humour, which had a great success with the relatively small 'reading public'. Torrente's national fame and wide recognition came with the televised version of *Los gozos y las sombras* in 1982. A series of major novels has appeared from the late 1970s to the present, the writer – enjoying a quiet life in Salamanca, but much in demand for TV appearances and interviews with journalists on literary matters – displaying astonishing vigour well on in his eighties. *The King Amaz'd* of 1989 is a sort of massive squib placed under the gilded chair occupied by any kind of established authority.

COLIN SMITH was Professor of Spanish at Cambridge until he took early retirement in 1990 in order to write and travel. His main interests are in Spanish medieval and Renaissance literature and history, the modern language including lexicography, and Romance philology, also recently in modern Galician writing. He translated Cunqueiro's *Merlin and Company* for the Everyman series.

A BRIEF CHRONOLOGY OF SPAIN
SINCE 1898

1898	Following war with the US, Spain loses her last American possessions: Cuba, Puerto Rico, Philippines.
1902	Alfonso XIII (born 1886) crowned.
1914–18	Spain neutral during First World War.
1923–9	Dictatorship of General Primo de Rivera.
1931	Municipal elections give victory to Republicans. Abdication of Alfonso XIII, creation of Second Republic.
1936–9	Civil War, resulting in victory by General Franco and his allies. In 1947, Spain was proclaimed a monarchy with a regency council and Franco as Caudillo (Leader) and head of state.
1939–45	Spain neutral during Second World War.
1946	Withdrawal of ambassadors to Spain by all UN nations.
1953	Spain makes defence agreement with US, allowing air and naval bases on her territory in return for economic aid.
1975	Death of Franco. Accession of King Juan Carlos I. Removal of most restrictions on free expression.
1975–7	Period of 'transition' to democracy. Elections in 1977 place a reforming centre-right government in power.
1981	Spain joins NATO.
1982	Elections give victory to the Socialist Party (PSOE).
1983	Agreement by which Spain is reconstituted as a state of seventeen autonomías (regional governments).
1986	Spain joins the European Union.
1990	World Cup (soccer) held in Spain.
1992	Olympic Games held in Barcelona.

INTRODUCTION

Gonzalo Torrente Ballester was born on 13 June 1910 in Ferrol in what is now the autonomous region of Galicia in north-west Spain. His father was a naval officer and the family lived in modest but happy enough circumstances, a prime factor (in relation to Gonzalo's career) being that it was a bookish household in which the boy was able to indulge his passion for reading everything he could lay his hands on, as he continued to do later in public and college libraries. His education followed the usual pattern of high school and the University of Santiago, where he took his history degree as an external student (the family being unable to finance his full-time internal residence) in 1935. With his family on the move, Gonzalo had begun an independent existence in Madrid in 1928 where his intellectual formation seems to have begun in earnest as he attended lectures on historical and philosophical subjects and frequented the *tertulias* (regular gatherings of friends) in the literary cafés of the capital. In 1932 he returned to Galicia and married, working as a humble teacher of Latin and philosophy in a private school, and becoming involved in the political movement for Galician autonomy which flourished under the Republic of 1931–6. Already, indeed from childhood, he essayed literary composition and was managing to read widely in classical and recent literature in several languages. Just before the outbreak of the Spanish Civil War in July 1936 he went to Paris in order to start work on a doctoral dissertation on a historical subject, but the distress caused by the war led him to return in difficult circumstances to Vigo in order to rejoin his family. He secured a temporary teaching post in Ferrol but left it at times to work as a journalist for Falangist publications (one of the few kinds allowed) in Pamplona and Burgos, and in 1938 he published his first play, both this and his work for magazines attracting the attention of the severe political censors of the day. By 1939 he was back in Santiago, and from 1942 to 1947 at his post in Ferrol, after which he lived in Madrid until 1964, writing plays which were not performed and novels which, while published, attracted little attention, and supporting himself by work on literary anthologies and editions and now by more extensive journalistic writings. He was, however, becoming steadily better known at least as a critic, especially of the theatre, and as author of surveys of recent and contemporary literature.

Torrente's first literary success came with the publication in 1957 of the first volume, *El señor llega (The Master Arrives)* of what was to be his 'Galician trilogy', the success lying not so much in critical acclaim – which was muted – as in the award of a generously endowed literary prize for the best novel of the preceding five years. The theme of the trilogy is Galician society and its tensions and struggles for power, personal and social and industrial, in the years preceding the Civil War. Any pleasure in this achievement was gravely affected by the tragic death of his wife Josefina in early 1958. Eventually Torrente recovered his energies and ambitions: he remarried (his second wife Fernanda eventually adding seven children to the four of the first marriage), and he worked rapidly on the rest of the trilogy, completed in 1962 under the title of *Los gozos y las sombras (Joys and Shadows)*. His struggles for recognition in the difficult literary world of Spain at the time were far from over, however: it was not simply a question of the Franquist censorship (he was, with many other intellectuals, in political trouble again in 1962, when he was banned from writing for the official newspapers and from broadcasting) but also of literary taste in the critical establishment and in the small reading public. At least it was clear that Torrente's future lay in the realm of the novel and not in the theatre. In 1963 he published his most ambitious work to date, *Don Juan*, on a theme which if it has beckoned temptingly to Spaniards since the original *burlador* (in one sense, seducer, in another, trickster) trod the stage in the early seventeenth century, has also proved perilous because of the comparisons a new work invites. Torrente's version is more intellectualized and theological than sensual. This again proved controversial even before publication. Janet Pérez records that 'Upon presentation in the censor's office, *Don Juan* was received with praise but drastically cut; one friar who found it "very good" proposed to excise 140 pages [it has only 347 in my edition]. The novelist sent the book to the then-minister Fraga Iribarne [Minister of Information and Tourism, later under democracy for long the leader of the principal right-wing party, and today President of the Autonomous Government of Galicia] – a former student of his – with the result that the minister authorized the complete, uncut version.' This was how matters had to be handled in those days, but it is now hard to see how even a friar could have been alarmed by the book to the extent that this one was. In 1964 the family moved to Pontevedra in Galicia, Torrente returning also to high-school teaching and apparently delighted to be in a place whose people and charms he celebrated, together with those of Santiago, in the mythical city he created later for the *Saga/fuga*.

Torrente's life changed greatly in 1966 when he accepted an invitation – made on whose inspired initiative is apparently not recorded – to become visiting professor in the State University of New York at Albany. There he worked happily until 1970, and less continuously for a further year or two, perhaps for the first time in his life free of financial worries and granted, more, the precious gifts of time and solitude in which to write, together with the presence of admiring colleagues and students devoted to him. In 1969 he published his lengthy novel *Off-side* (544 pages), a dense tale of recent and contemporary Madrid society in its intellectual, artistic, and also sexual aspects considered against a background of high finance and not so high politics. There is also here a substantial adumbration of the question which was to preoccupy Torrente greatly in later work: the relation of the artist to his creation, of author to character. While in the US he prepared a good deal of the *Saga/fuga*, using now a tape-recorder in order to save his always extremely weak eyesight. The elaborate and often difficult process of creation is documented in *Cuadernos de La Romana* (1975) – that is 'jottings in notebooks' made in the house in La Romana, a section of a small town near Vigo where he bought a property on his return from America. Torrente had no pressing reason to abandon his American university experience – which, as shown repeatedly in later works, marked and stimulated him most agreeably – other than concern for his ailing mother and feeling (stronger in Galicians than in any other people, it seems) for his homeland. It is hard to imagine the *Saga/fuga* being conceived by anyone who was not resident there at least in the spirit.

La saga/fuga de J.B. was published in 1972. (The title has no ready translation: *Saga* is obviously 'saga', a long heroic tale; *fuga* is both 'fugue', that species of musical composition which returns repeatedly, with variations, to a theme, and also 'fleeing, flight', in this case that of the protagonist at the end of the literary construct.) It is a work of 585 pages – uncommitted and faint-hearted readers are said to reach page 60 repeatedly and give up the effort – and is by far Torrente's greatest book. The present translator recalls with gratitude the kindly suggestion by Emilio Lorenzo, the doyen of English studies in Spain, made at the bookshop of the small Santander airport in 1973, that this novelty was worth acquiring. Rather more than that, it has changed his life, to the extent that this translator is known to Torrente as 'that Cambridge madman who reads the *Saga/fuga* once every year' as is perfectly true. On publication the work did have a considerable success in Spain, more especially among intellectuals and the truly bookish than with the public at large, probably, for although vastly humorous it is also extremely dense in its structure, its shifting perspective, its richness of allusion, and its woefully unparagraphed prose. As with *Don Quixote* and *Tristram Shandy* (both, with Joyce, being by no means irrelevant mentions here), it is really extremely hard to say what the book is 'about'. The narrator, the J.B. of the title, is José Bastida, a humble and, in contemporary Franquist terms, politically dubious schoolmaster of the mythical, self-inventing and eventually self-levitating Galician city Castroforte del Baralla, who realizes with growing concern that he is (with two other J.B. contemporaries) the last in line of a series of persons from early Antiquity onward, all having the initials J.B., whose mission it has been and is 'to save the city'. These are paralleled and opposed by clerics whose names all begin with *A*, and paralleled and (in some cases) distracted by women whose names begin with *C* and who maintain a dotty but ineradicable ritual of mystical eroticism. On the one hand myths about the city's origins and history, its famous river lampreys, its select families, its parrot which holds the collective memory of the place, its ecclesiastical traditions, its holy relic, are erected and explored and embellished, while on the other hand they are dissected and queried and rejected in a perpetual dialectic which involves 'outside' personages such as a 'full-professor' of local origins but domiciled in the US who returns to engage in the controversy. All this is set against a background in which the native Galicians or 'Celts' of Castroforte, liberals and anticlericals by tradition who receive dangerous books and doctrines by sea from abroad, oppose and sometimes manage to outwit the 'Goths' from outside who occupy positions of power as representatives of the Madrid authorities. (One can see that by 1972 the Franquist censorship, which must have perceived a wealth of contemporary allusions in the book, had greatly softened its policies; so far as is known, the work was published unchanged.) On another plane, however, Castroforte, documented for us only in the fertile brain of its chronicler J.B., is happy in its non-existence, neglected by all-powerful national authorities because it figures on no known map. As J.B. narrates and speculates and invents, from his vantage-point of official scribe to the members of the 'Round Table' of like-minded local intellectuals (bearing Arthurian names) all manner of contemporary disciplines and modes of thought are wheeled in and applied parodically to the myths and situations under review, so that we have subversive lessons in structuralist analysis, linguistics, literary theory, sociology, Freudian psychology, and much else, while the whole book with its ever-shifting perspectives and chaotic reversals of time is a parody of the *nouveau roman*. There is constant questioning also of the nature of written and oral-tradition evidence from the past which defines that past for us: the joking hoaxer is really no different from the self-interested falsifier and the inspired myth-maker, and poets (there is a classic late-Romantic one here) equally in their posthumously hyped-up lives and in their verses are specially dangerous witnesses. For some readers and researchers there is the additional pleasure of recognizing, in what is apparently a *roman à clef*, characters drawn from the life among the author's friends from his Santiago and Pontevedra days. One salutes what must surely be the best humorous creation in Spanish since Cervantes, and recalls that it is no accident that at the time of its composition Torrente was working on a brief but extremely perceptive study which he published as *El Quijote como juego* ('The *Quixote* as a game' or 'as playfulness') in 1975. The English adjective 'Cervantick' (rather than more neutral 'Cervantine') has the right kind of resonances for it to be properly applied to the *Saga/fuga*. A large part of its success with critics must have been owed to the fact that here was a native work which could be set beside the products of the great Latin-American 'boom' with its discovery and exploitation of 'magic realism', though Torrente has denied that his book is a parody of García Márquez's *Cien años de soledad* (1967) on the very reasonable grounds that he had not read it at the time. It would not be beyond the writer's ability, however, to write a parody-by-anticipation.

In 1977 Torrente published a further very interesting novel, *Fragmentos de apocalipsis*, and in 1980 *La isla de los jacintos cortados*, both of which are in a way further explorations of inventive literary techniques and narrative theory, now on a more serious plane but far from devoid of humorous notes. The decade of the 1980s has seen the writer in astonishingly productive form, in part with new narratives, in part as essayist and literary critic (much of his earlier, scattered production now being anthologized), while publishers have been found for re-issues of early plays and novels for so long unregarded. Torrente in this late flowering and time of genuinely widespread public recognition has participated a good deal in radio and television

interviews and discussions, being now an extremely senior guru
of marvellously sound sense, uncomplicated language, and high
good humour, an excellent communicator in his very quiet and
modest way, esteemed by all. He lives in Salamanca, appropri-
ately enough, since this is Spain's oldest university town. He has
received many literary prizes, and since 1975 has been a member
of the prestigious Royal Spanish Academy of the Language.
While literary historians seem to date the overdue public recognition of Torrente as a major writer to 1972 when the *Saga/fuga*
was published, in my experience this is not accurate. The book
enjoyed a notable *succès d'estime*, it is true, but wider public
recognition was owed to the very competent television series –
thirteen episodes – made of the trilogy *Los gozos y las sombras*
and broadcast from March 1982. This was a native 'first' for
Spanish TV, not precisely in nature but certainly in quality, since
in that line it had hitherto imported and dubbed such foreign
products as famous BBC series. As happened also in Britain (for
example with the Galsworthy *Forsyte Saga* or now, 1994 and
1995, George Eliot's *Middlemarch* and Jane Austen's *Pride and
Prejudice*), a major TV success leads at once to curiosity about
the original author and a rush to read the book and then others
by the same hand, with the difference that in Torrente's case, in
Spain, he was in the early 1980s still very much alive and
apparently able to take heart from all this and to generate new
energies. Recent novels of great originality include *Quizá nos
lleve el viento al infinito* (1984) and *Yo no soy yo, evidentemente*
(1987), in which earlier preoccupations with the nature of
authorship and of the literary personage are still being worked
out.

This happy state of affairs continues. The *Crónica del rey
pasmado* of 1989, when the author was aged seventy-eight, no
less, is unlike anything Torrente had essayed before. It is in one
way a very plain narrative, in others a richly ironical view of the
attitudes and institutions and persons of a period which for
most Spaniards is set in memoristic amber as something classical
and untouchable. One suspects that the writer's inspiration for
it came at a moment when he was viewing one of the great

pictures of the time, a range of which is mentioned below, and out of his feeling that gorgeous dresses and facial masks and signs of authority could be stripped away in order to see what kinds of day-to-day human reality might lie beneath, not in any savage spirit of upending the historical and pictorial record, but with humour and gentle irony; though it is really rather daring of him to suggest that in a period of intense and utterly conformist religiosity, the devil was fairly freely at work in an altogether beneficent and undevilish way. The *Crónica* was published by Editorial Planeta in Barcelona, and by September 1992 was in its nineteenth printing, having sold over 150,000 copies.

In 1991 a film was made of the book, with the author's collaboration so far as the script was concerned, and was a considerable success in the cinema and as a video. It was directed by Imanol Uribe and had the veteran actor Fernando Fernán Gómez in the role of Chief Inquisitor. It is not, alas, fully satisfactory. To mention three shortcomings: in the film the wealth of allusion to literary persons and to pictures is lost, the debates in the Council of the Inquisition are greatly truncated, and more grievously, what are in the book the dark labyrinthine passageways of the old palace are represented as large brightly lit parts of a neoclassical building. Doubtless the cinema and the telefilm are the prime art of our times, in the public esteem, but the printed word of the novelistic page may still say more to the imagination.

It has not been easy to find a single word which would adequately represent the *pasmado* of the original. This has a wide range which includes 'thunderstruck', 'astonished', 'speechless with awe', 'bewildered', 'agape', and so on. I have settled for *The King Amaz'd: A Chronicle*, in the hope that this will strike the right note, but readers who contemplate imaginatively, through the King's eyes, the back of the sleeping Marfisa, may come up with a different version.

COLIN SMITH

THE SETTING OF *THE KING AMAZ'D*

For Spanish readers of the original having some slight acquaintance with the history and art of their nation, the identification
of the characters and setting of Torrente Ballester's story will
have caused no problem. Others may welcome a hint or two.

We are in the early 1620s. The King, unnamed in the story, is
Philip IV of Spain, born on 8 April 1605. He came to the throne
on 31 March 1621 on the death of his father Philip III, and was
to reign till 1665. The Queen, also unnamed, is Isabel de
Bourbon, better known to the Spaniards as Isabel de Francia,
elder daughter of Henry IV of France ('*le Béarnais*'), born
22 November 1602. They were betrothed in 1612 and married
on 18 October 1615, but the marriage was not allowed to be
consummated until November 1620 when Isabel was eighteen
(and Philip only fifteen).

There is frequent mention of the ways in which divine wrath
might be visited upon the Spaniards. The English under Lord
Wimbledon (Sir Edward Cecil) attacked Spanish shipping in
the Bay of Cadiz and made a landing there in 1625. This was
not mere privateering, since the expedition consisted of nine
thousand men and a fleet of ninety ships. As for the war in
Flanders, it was more or less a constant during the period, but
the image of it which Spanish readers would most readily call
to mind is Velázquez's great painting known to them as *La
rendición de Breda (The Surrender of Breda)* or *Las lanzas (The
Lances*: the event was of 1625, the painting probably of 1629)
which occupies its own heroic space in the Prado Museum,
Madrid.

Philip's Chief Minister, in the Spanish original *el Valido*
('the Favourite'), is Don Gaspar de Guzmán, Conde-Duque de
Olivares, who held his post from 1621 to 1643. His wife is

his cousin Inés de Zúñiga y Velasco (in the story, 'Lady Barbara').

The various ecclesiastics in the story do not appear to have any well-known prototypes in history, but are none the less authentic for that.

One figure at court who can be identified because she is fully named in the story is Doña Francisca de Távora, recorded in history largely because the King (a noted and sometimes spectacular womanizer) was said to have had an affair with her.

The men who are exchanging the news and gossip of the day in a period virtually without newspapers or other equivalents of the modern media might be thought merely typical and anonymous, but enough clues are given for several of them to be identified. 'Don Luis', the author of the scurrilous *décima* (ten-line stanza), is Luis de Góngora (1562–1627), the greatest poet of the day. His *Polifemo* and *Soledades* of 1611–13 brought him such fame that he moved from his native Cordova to Madrid with a sinecure as royal chaplain, an official post which in no way diminished his instinct to compose satirical verse. His poem about Marfisa is securely dated to 1624. The man with the spectacles who berates the bystanders for their frivolity is Francisco de Quevedo (1580–1645), a satirist who in verse and prose was at least Góngora's equal (and at times a bitter enemy of his in the war of words) and a writer of genius in many genres. The gentleman depicted with his hand on his breast is the nameless subject of El Greco's portrait *El caballero de la mano al pecho*, who would have been a good age by this time because he was painted at some date between 1577 and 1584. The 'talking-shop' (in the original *el mentidero* or 'place of lying') had a specific location, the steps of the church of San Felipe in the Calle Mayor in central Madrid. The old palace stood on the western edge of the capital on a low cliff overlooking the Campo del Moro and the Manzanares river (this is the site of the present palace, built in the nineteenth century). It had been built into the old Moorish fortress and still had features of that. In 1632 Olivares had a fine new palace built for the monarch in what is now the Retiro park. Streets and gates and churches mentioned in the story can be identified on the modern map of the city.

The paintings of the time are indeed the clue to much that happens in the story. *La rendición de Breda* has already been mentioned. The King's indecision at the end about who should be nominated as the new court painter was in historical terms resolved by bringing from Seville the young Diego Velázquez. A number of famous paintings of his are dated to the early and mid-1620s in which the story is set. He painted the King, the Queen, and their children on many occasions, and other personages and scenes at intervals. His portraits of the Conde-Duque convey much of the awesome power which the man enjoyed in life, and his grim dedication to his duties. In 1622 he painted Góngora, the admirable original being now in Boston (there are two fair early copies in Spain), and Quevedo about the same time, with spectacles (the original is lost but a copy survives). Among several pictures in this period of gentlemen with crosses (of the Order of Calatrava) on their breasts at least one by Velázquez is known. The convent of San Plácido may well have come to Torrente Ballester's mind not merely because it was there in Madrid at the time but for a particular painterly reason: Velázquez's extraordinary *Crucifixion* was painted about 1632 for this convent of Benedictine nuns and until 1800 was in their sacristy. It was said to have been commissioned by the King in expiation of his sin in having sacrilegiously seduced a nun of the convent.

And the Velázquez nude displayed ('detail' only, as the art books say) on the cover of the book? The Spaniards call this the *Venus del espejo*, 'Venus and the Mirror'. It was painted in the 1640s, apparently before 1648 when Velázquez went to Italy for the second time (though some have claimed it was painted there). It was commissioned by the grandee Gaspar Menéndez de Haro, and passed to the Alba family by marriage in 1688. In 1802 Charles IV ordered that it and other works should be sold to his favourite, Godoy, on whose fall from power in 1808 it was sold via agents and eventually (on the advice of Sir Thomas Lawrence) purchased by Mr Morritt for £500 for his collection at Rokeby Hall in Yorkshire, whence its designatioin as 'the Rokeby Venus'. It was acquired for the National Gallery in 1906. The name of Velázquez's model is not known, of course: a peasant girl, a serving-maid, a prostitute (since such a one might sell her services in this way as in others), who can say? Torrente's sardonic inspiration would have it otherwise. Towards the end of the story, the Queen is shown trying on immensely elaborate dresses of the kind she is indeed wearing in several portraits of her. These extend from chin to floor in a sort of downward pyramidal shape and conceal everything except face and hands. Ah yes, chuckles Torrente, but we who are now absorbed as active and implicit readers within his story now know, don't we, which liberated lady (liberated in ways outlined in the story) was really the model – back view only, naturally – for this greatest of paintings of the nude. Delicacy of feelings together with plain political prudence preserved the royal anonymity, of course: the face is fuzzy and out of focus because the way Cupid is holding the mirror to it makes it useless – that is, for purposes of identification – from where the viewer of the picture is standing. Never, one feels, has the phrase (invented by another royal person) *Honi soit qui mal y pense* been better applied . . . But of course, if Marfisa did reach Italy (as in the story she intends), and if Velázquez did after all paint the picture there, we have a different solution, and the view granted to the beholder of the picture is precisely that which at the start of the story left the King, well, amaz'd.

THE KING AMAZ'D

A CHRONICLE

CHAPTER ONE

I

The early morning of that Sunday in October was rich in miracles, marvels, and surprises, although as always the witnesses and bits of evidence were not in full accord. It would indeed be more exact to say that everybody was talking about the events but nobody had seen them. Still, since such agreement can never be achieved, it is best to leave matters just as people told and still tell them. One incontrovertible piece of evidence was the hole which opened up in the Calle del Pez: it remained open to the inspection of all throughout the day, and people came to see it and to smell it, as if it were a rhinoceros. The affair as it is related went something like this: early in the morning an old woman saw a snake emerge from beneath a stone; the snake made off downhill (the same way it might have made off uphill); but what the saddle-maker in the Calle de San Roque saw was no longer a snake, but more of a serpent, which also made off, uphill or downhill, the report does not say. The devout old dear who emerged from early Mass at San Ginés saw a huge great serpent which she was sure was heading for the palace, more or less, and finally, what a soldier of the Walloon Guard who was going on duty or just coming from it (this point is not fully clear) saw with astonished or disoriented eyes was a gigantic boa constrictor which completely surrounded the palace at ground level, and appeared to be squeezing the building with the idea of demolishing it, or at least of compressing it, which seems more likely and makes better sense. The soldier began to shout in his own language, but, since nobody could understand him, this gave time for the huge beast to give up his attempt, or so it seemed, and to glide off in a calm and sinister way towards

the Campo del Moro, where he was hunted in vain all morning
by teams of experts organized in hourly shifts. The business
about the cache of ancient coins was credited to a child's good
fortune, but it was said to have been found in different spots:
according to some, outside the Ambassadors' Gate, on the right
as you come out; according to others, near the Puerta de Toledo,
on the left as you come out. Neither the boy nor the treasure
was heard of again.

Of course, everybody heard the bells of Santa Agueda ringing
on their own; but – who is 'everybody'? As for desperate shrieks
coming from a ruined house, that was in the Las Vistillas
quarter. They were loud, agonized shrieks, as might come from
those condemned to everlasting fire or the like, though they
might also have come from souls doing penance in Purgatory.
They were, by all accounts, extremely distressing. What could
readily be checked by anyone who cared to do so was the thing
in the Calle del Pez. There was indeed a big hole there which
crossed the street in an irregular line from south to north. What
emerged from the hole (from the chasm, according to the first
witnesses, now unknown) appeared to be sulphurous gases, on
account of which everyone thought, rightly, that down in the
depths of the hole was where hell began, especially bearing in
mind that together with the gases there emerged roars of pain
and frightful blasphemous oaths. However, when people began
to gather and discuss the matter, there was no longer any chasm,
and it smelled no worse than the street usually did. Evidently
the gases had dispersed.

2

Don Secundino Mirambel Pacheco, the parish priest of San
Martín, the one with a cloak, had been in the Indies as a young
man, and from one of the voyages had brought back a spyglass
given him by a Genoese pilot he had become friendly with
during the crossing. Each night, if the sky was reasonably clear
and the stars could be made out with sufficient clarity, Don

Secundino scanned the heavens. For a long while Don Secundino was considered no more than a competent amateur star-gazer, when he talked about heavenly bodies with his friends while they drank their chocolate in the afternoons, and the same by his relatives; but most people did not care to concern themselves with astronomical questions beyond what the preachers advised, and these generally used the stars as an example of the love which the Divinity had for beauty, and again as an example of obedience, since the stars moved in accordance with orders laid down for them many centuries before, and it was not known how many centuries that might be, nor was it proper to speculate about it. One night, however, one Saturday night, Don Secundino saw through his spyglass not only stars but witches too, and thought it best to report his discovery to the Inquisition. After a secret session, the Inquisitor-General in person charged Don Secundino with the duty of preparing a weekly report on the nature and number of the witches he observed, and of any warlocks too who might be flying over the city on a Saturday night, even though this might serve merely to keep the statistics in order. That Sunday morning, a mild and sunny one, Don Secundino drew up his weekly report in his conscientious way and in the elegant prose of one who had been nurtured on the best Latin classics and had learned his Spanish in the neighbour-hood of Ecija (if he lisped a bit like any Andalusian, the lisp would not appear on paper). He left his house in the cool of early morning, handed his report to a manservant of the Inquisition, and after saying Mass and having a cup of chocolate with a glass of water, for his health, he went home. There he lay down without undressing, since on Sundays and just in case, he was in the habit of taking a nap. The servant of the Holy Office took the report to the Inquisitor-General, who had been up from early morning, with Mass already said and grave problems in his heart and in his head. He was in his room next to the Great Hall of the Council. He opened Don Secundino's report and glanced at it. Then something caught his attention and he began to read it intently, frowning the while and from time to time uttering such exclamations as:

'God be with us! So it's come to this! The devil's out on the loose!'

3

Count de la Peña Andrada was putting the finishing touches to his coiffure, looking into a mirror which Lucretia had brought him. She was watching him from behind, watching both him and his reflection in the mirror. When the Count put the comb down, she planted a kiss on his hair and purred: 'Very handsome!' Then she brought him his sky-blue doublet so that he could finish dressing.

'Has your mistress woken up yet?'

'She's pretty lazy, specially on Sundays.'

'Then we'll have to wake the King. It's high time already.'

'I wouldn't dare to, my lord. You do it.'

They went over to the door of Marfisa's room, and Lucretia opened it, taking care to make no noise. A sunbeam crossed the room, lighting up the big wooden floor tiles, red and white, and stretching over to the very edge of the bed. In the shadows two sleeping figures could be made out: the King, on the nearer edge, and Marfisa, further over. The Count went across on tiptoe and touched the King's bare shoulder.

'My lord, it's time now.'

His Majesty opened his eyes languidly.

'What? What's that?'

'It's time to get up. It's late already.'

A clock in a tower was beginning to chime eight o'clock. The bells reverberated in the warm air, spread their sound, mingled one with another, until it seemed there was simply one big peal.

'Surely it's too early, Count?'

'We have to cross the city.'

'On foot?'

'I hope my coach will be waiting for us.'

The King sat up in bed. Unclothed he looked very thin, and

seemed to have fragile bones. He pushed the blanket aside and sat completely naked.

'Bring me my clothes.'

The Count did so in silence. The King began to dress.

'I could do with a bit of refreshment.'

'I'm sure something can be found, Your Majesty.'

Marfisa's body was half on view: her hair, her back, her slim waist, part of her bottom. The King looked at her in surprise, in rapt amazement.

'Have you ever seen anything lovelier?'

'There are many lovely things in the world.'

'Lovelier than a woman's body?'

'If it's Marfisa's, hardly.'

'Until last night, I had never seen a woman naked.'

'So?'

'Paradise must be something like this.'

The Count scowled.

'I doubt if the gentlemen of the Inquisition would approve of that notion.'

'And what can the gentlemen of the Inquisition know about naked women?'

'According to them, everything.'

The King was half dressed now. The Count asked Lucretia for a basin of cold water. The King began to poke about in his pouch.

'Your Majesty is looking for something?'

'Yes, that half-ducat to leave for Marfisa.'

'Just a half-ducat?'

'That is the amount fixed by protocol, I believe.'

The Count smiled.

'Your Majesty, that protocol is out of date, and Marfisa is the most expensive whore in town. At least ten ducats.'

The King looked at him in surprise.

'I don't have ten ducats. I have never had ten ducats. This half-ducat I'm looking for – I had to beg that from my valet. Afterwards, you know, they go off and put it in their memoirs.'

The Count put his hand in his pouch and drew out a velvet purse.

'There's ten ducats. They were going to be Lucretia's.'

Lucretia came in with the bowl and heard what the Count had just said.

'Your Lordship has no reason to give me anything. I consider myself well paid.'

The King looked at the Count, and the Count smiled again.

'Well', said the King, 'Marfisa didn't say that to me.'

'The fact is, Your Majesty, that my mistress does it as a profession, and I ... well, I do it just for love, and the Count amply satisfied me.'

'You may kiss her in my presence, Count.'

The King splashed his face with water and dried it with the towel Lucretia held out to him. He put on his hat, but the Count kept his in his hand.

'Put your hat on, Count,' said the King.

The Count obeyed.

'I thank you, Your Majesty.'

'We'll do the same in the palace, in the presence of the Chief Minister, just to give him a fit. Now, let's go.'

Lucretia went with them to the door. She gave the Count a kiss and whispered 'He-man' in his ear. The coach was waiting: nothing sumptuous, but solid and elegant. Lucretia waved to them. The coach rattled off along the street, which was full of pot-holes. The King stared straight ahead, as if lost in the infinite. There was a sort of dazed look on his face.

'What are you looking at so intently, Your Majesty?'

'Marfisa's body. I can't see anything else.'

4

The valet who had lent the King half a ducat entered the office through the secret door, and stood still, humbly, but looking at the Chief Minister out of the corner of his eye.

'Was there something, Cosme?'

'Put two and two together, Excellency. His Majesty did not sleep in the palace; his bed has not been slept in, and he is nowhere to be found. Yesterday, when I left him, he asked me for half a ducat.'

'And what do you deduce from that, Cosme?'

'That the King went out whoring. Excellency: half a ducat is what monarchs pay their whores, as I have always heard tell.'

'There are things, Cosme, that one should never hear.'

'I beg your pardon, Excellency, but thanks to the fact that I am not deaf, Your Excellency receives me in secret.'

'You're right, Cosme. And did the King go out alone?'

'I don't rightly know. But when I left him, Count de la Peña Andrada was with him.'

The Chief Minister thought for a moment, gazing at the frieze on the opposite wall where it joined the ceiling panels. A mad romp of sphinxes and many-headed dragons, beautifully carved.

'Count de la Peña Andrada. And who might he be?'

'I could not say, sir, only that he is a young gentleman, very handsome, and that the King is on intimate terms with him.'

'You may go, Cosme. Thanks.'

Cosme bowed and went out through the same door as he had entered by. The Chief Minister rang his little bell: a gentle sound, but a penetrating one. An usher came in and stood silently next to the door. The Chief Minister wrote a few words on a paper.

'Take this to the head archivist and have him bring me what I'm asking him for at once.'

The usher departed. The Chief Minister muttered: 'So he went off whoring and I knew nothing about it?'

The Minister's face did not look very happy, and his eyes were anxious. The head archivist soon arrived.

'This is what you were asking for, Your Excellency.'

'Did you have much trouble finding it?'

'None at all, Your Excellency. It was on my table.'

'Why would it have been there? Has this Count recently sent in some request?'

'So far as I recall, no, Your Excellency. It's a name I had never

heard. Count de la Peña Andrada ... It's all very odd. And
yet ...'

'And yet, what?'

'There you have his papers. Everything in order; it's a title
granted by the Emperor, a personal title, but declared to be
hereditary and valid in Castile by His Majesty Philip II, who
also granted the holders of the title privateering rights against
Englishmen and Hollanders, on condition that they maintain a
squadron of six ships and hand over to the Crown one fifth of
the prize-money. Their accounts are in order, my lord, and they
have paid over to the Crown a useful amount in coin and other
valuables. There is also ...' (the head archivist paused and
looked at the Minister) 'there is also a lawsuit against the house
of Andrada, concerning property boundaries. What is in dispute
is the Valdoviño valley. The case is with the Royal Chancellery
at Valladolid.'

'And that Valdoviño place, where might it be?'

'It must be up Galicia way, my lord. A land full of witches,
where you can't see anything plain. People from up there who
are of any worth either come to Madrid, as the Lemos family
did, or stay in Salamanca, like the Monterrey clan. In this
lawsuit there is mention of villages and towns nobody ever
heard of: Cedeira, Santa María de Ortigueira ... and somewhere called Caraño or Cariño, it's not very clear. They're the
harbours authorized for that squadron ...'

The Chief Minister looked at the fat dossier, and picked it up.

'Papers, more papers. You keep them, my good sir, but don't
lose sight of them. I may need them.'

The archivist picked up the file, bowed, bowed again at the
door, and went out. His departure coincided with the arrival of
Father Germán de Villaescusa, a Capuchin, who came in by the
secret door. He bowed deeply. The Minister rose and kissed his
hand.

'You know about this business, Father?'

'The whole palace knows about it. The King has just got
back. He said not a word, just went off to his rooms, sat down
at a window, and appears to be contemplating the heavens.'

'Signs of repentance?'

'How can one interpret the look of a man who is staring at the horizon?'

'In a thousand ways: half of them goodly, half evil.'

'This man is the King.'

'Who has just spent the night in the embrace of sinfulness.'

'So it would seem, Father, and that's the trouble.'

'Does Your Excellency have any other details?'

'That the pimp was a certain Count de la Peña Andrada, who is not known to me.'

'I, on the other hand, have heard that name . . . yes, let me think. He's a Galician, I believe?'

'It seems so.'

'The presence of the Apostle St James in that region does not seem to further the Saviour's cause. I know with absolute certainty that more than ninety per cent of the Galicians, clergy included, are damned.'

'Isn't that a big number, Father?'

'There may be some error, but it can only be a small one. Let's leave it at eighty-nine per cent.'

'Even so . . .'

'The women . . . those who aren't witches are whores. Reports made to the Holy Office confirm it.'

'There ought to be some way by which His Majesty, without relinquishing the lands, could be free of such people.'

'I don't think that should be too difficult . . .'

The Minister had a vision of the remote Kingdom of Galicia afire on all four sides, in some gigantic auto-da-fé. Father Villaescusa's remedies were always the same.

They said nothing for a moment, and looked at each other.

'The problem is, Father, that we are expecting the arrival of a fleet from the Indies, and then again, it seems that a major battle is imminent in the Low Countries.'

The priest crossed himself.

'If the English steal our gold and the Dutch make off with the victory, we shall have to bow before the will of God.'

'Yes, Father, of course. But God's will is not inflexible.'

The priest stood up.

'I will go and pray, to see if the Lord will inspire me with some solution. It's early yet. There's still two hours to go before High Mass. What may one not receive from God in that time!'

'Then please remember me in your prayers, Father. Two days ago, my wife began her period . . .'

'That is a harsh burden that women have to bear, one which serves to mark their inferior position with regard to men.'

The Minister stood up, went across to the priest, and put his hands on his shoulders.

'But I need an heir, Father, I need that more than my own life, a life which must not be extinguished when I die. You, Father, know all about my prayers and my sacrifices. It seems the Lord will not listen to us, neither to my wife nor to myself.'

'Perhaps your prayers are not reaching heaven.'

'Do you want us to shout them out, Father? Shout in public, dress up as penitents, stop eating and drinking?'

'I can give you no answer, my lord. I am going to say my prayers. The Most High will grant me some sort of inspiration.'

He bowed again, more briefly than before, and went out through the secret door.

5

When Marfisa shouted the third time Lucretia went to her. She really hadn't shouted as much as she did most mornings, when the whole neighbourhood could hear her.

'Lucretia, Lucretia, you she-devil, wherever were you hiding?'

Lucretia came in with a contrite air.

'I was preparing my lady's bath.'

'Ah, splendid idea. It's just what my body needs, a good bath, but not too hot. What sort of a day is it?'

'It's warm, my lady, but you could be out in the yard in the shade of the vine arbour. It seems summer is still with us.'

Marfisa was spreadeagled naked on the bed, with the sheets

around her feet all knotted up, as though she had been kicking them.

'What about those two fellows?'

'They left very early, madam.'

'Did they seem satisfied?' Then, before Lucretia could answer, she added: 'Did they pay you?'

'There's a purse on the table with ten ducats in gold, and the King gave me half a ducat. I think that was all he had on him.'

She handed the money to Marfisa, who jingled the coins.

'Well, at least it's gold. Ten ducats, did you say? That works out at two-and-a-half for each crime against Our Lord, with the purse as a gratuity. It's a nice velvet one.'

'Did my lady say as a gratuity?'

'Yes, darling, there was nothing doing the fifth time. He got stuck with looking at me and then looking me all over again, and when he got tired of that, he said he was sleepy and left me wanting more. Just when I was getting to like the idea. How about you?'

'I spent the night in pure pleasure, my lady, with the Count permanently on top of me, looking at me all the time with those cat's eyes of his. Cat's eyes, no ... more like a tiger's. A tiger's eyes must be something like that. They lit up the whole room.'

'Come off it!'

'I swear it on my mother's soul. She was a whore too, but repented in time. We gave her a jolly fine funeral, thanks be to God and to some generous Christian friends!'

'Leave your mother's soul out of it, and pass me a towel so that I can wrap up. While I'm bathing, get some lunch ready. I'm dying of hunger.'

She leaped out of bed and wrapped herself in the towel which Lucretia had got out of a chest. Her dark, tight-fleshed thighs and long legs were uncovered. Lucretia studied her.

'I now see why things are as they are and not as they ought to be. That body of yours deserved a better fate.'

'You mean I should have had a husband?'

'God forbid! No, I meant better lovers.'

'Does the King seem such a small catch, even though it was just for the one night?'

'The King did not leave you satisfied, to judge from what I've just heard. I, on the other hand . . .'

Marfisa answered her as Lucretia was leaving the room: 'The King's just a novice. He's not half with it yet, and he had never seen a woman naked. Just imagine what he'd learn in my bed on a seven nights' course, no more!'

'In that case, what's the point of his being King?'

6

The King stopped gazing at the horizon, from which the last naked woman had vanished, and sat for a few moments with his head down but with an expression of deep shock on his face. Then he rose and said to Cosme, who was waiting by the door: 'Bring me the keys of the secret room.'

Cosme trembled visibly.

'You heard.'

'What do I do if they refuse to hand them over?'

'Tell them it's a royal order.'

The valet bowed deeply and went out. For a time the King hesitated. He crossed to the open window which looked out on to the parade-ground. On the far side a squad of soldiers was drilling. Nearer, a few gentlemen were chatting, and a richly plumed rider was making his horse prance before an admiring group of spectators. All this under a sun which was beginning to be fierce. Someone spotted the King, and saluted him, doffing his hat. The others then saluted too, and the squad of soldiers presented arms. But the King did not see them: all he could see was an immense void, with no precise limits, as if it consisted of vapour. Yet the sky was clear. The King shut his eyes, and could still see it, whereupon he felt convinced that the void was inside himself, that that was all there was to see. He inwardly gazed upon it with his face motionless, staring straight ahead, until the usher returned and jangled the keys. The King turned and held out his hand.

The usher, kneeling to present them, said: 'I had to steal them, my lord.'

'Quite right too.'

The King went out with the keys, their jingling seeming to fill the semi-darkness. He crossed room after room, went down corridors, and with the largest key opened the largest door, which he then locked from within. He was now in a labyrinth of zigzagging passages, with every so often stairs going up and others going down. He still had to open two further doors, which he also locked after passing through them. The secret room was in a tower, the one on the north-east. It was in darkness. Feeling his way, he found a window and opened it. The room was unfurnished but there were pictures on the walls. As his eyes adjusted to the scant light, he could see that in all the pictures there were naked women, alone or accompanied. He was in the presence of the mythological canvases which his grandfather had collected, those that could be viewed only under special licence issued from the office of the Archbishop of Toledo, signed in the Primate's very own hand, a privilege of the Primate which the Inquisitor-General was challenging, leading to a suit which after some decades was still (being one of those that are never concluded) with the Roman curia. It was lucky that another monarch, his father, had never penetrated into that place, for if he had, the lawsuit would have been resolved by committing the pictures to the flames.

'The sharpest theologians, Your Majesty, have their doubts about whether your grandfather the Emperor attained salvation, simply because he spent the nation's money on those filthy things.'

The filthy things were signed by, among others, Titian, and a very rum Hollander known as *El Bosco*, 'Hierombosc', according to letters sent by the Emperor to his beloved daughters. The King let his eye rove over the accumulated bodies exposed to the elements and paused at a picture in which an old procuress was gathering in the folds of her skirt the gold which Zeus was aiming at Danae's crotch. Danae herself was still getting some gold where it mattered, apparently, to judge by her expression. Danae had long thighs and a burnished body, just like Marfisa. The King stood gazing at the picture for a long time, utterly rapt.

7

Brother Eugenio de Rivadesella arrived quite out of breath, or at least that is what he said, since it had not occurred to the Saint who founded his Order to devise a lighter habit for hot days, and the Inquisitor-General was obliged to recognize that his visitor was suffocating and to call urgently for some efficacious cooling drink to be brought, from the stock of such things kept for these emergencies deep in the well. Having drunk it, together with a glass of brandy as a chaser, Father Rivadesella became more sociable, though he continued to smell of sweat, which the Inquisitor found offensive. Still, he offered it up as a sacrifice counting towards the remission of his sins, and handed over to the friar the text of the report which the parish priest of San Pedro had brought him that same morning.

'What does Your Reverence think of this news?'

What was known in the higher circles of the Church and the Inquisition about Father Rivadesella was that every evening, as the light faded, he received a visit from the Evil One and held pleasurable converse with him, the results of this being applied later to the greater glory of God and of the monarchy. Father Rivadesella put his glasses on (brought to him by someone from Holland, where they had been made by heretics for sure, but at least keen-sighted ones) and concentrated on reading the report, not raising his eyes until he got to the last line. It was as well that the parish priest's cramped handwriting was clear and legible.

'I sent for you so early, Reverend Father, so that I could hear your views of what is said in those papers. You are the only person in the city whose opinion I can trust, given your well-known friendship with the Enemy of the human race and of Our Lord God.'

'I would not call it friendship, Your Excellency, more of a mere acquaintanceship.' His glasses now in his hand, playing with them, Father Rivadesella added: 'I must say first, Excellency, that this is the first news I have received of these happenings. It is however the case that yesterday evening, at twilight, Satan failed to turn up to an appointment with me. I usually wait for him under a holm-oak tree in our courtyard, which has such spreading foliage that it hides everything: I sit down under it and nobody can see a cross nor even the shadow of one. Satan would feel uncomfortable with either, you see. Well, he didn't turn up yesterday, even though I waited till it was fully dark, savouring the smoke of that herb they bring from the Indies. Tobacco, you know. I recommend it for troubled times.'

He spent some minutes singing the praises of tobacco and urging its use. Then he went on: 'I must say it's very odd, Excellency, and worth bearing in mind, that this morning, at the first light of dawn, a terrifying dragon with at least seven heads – maybe more – should have wrapped itself around the foundations of the palace with the idea of pulling it down, according to statements from eye-witnesses, and as everybody in the city already knows. There has been talk too of other prodigies, though of lesser account. My confidant Satan – who tells me many things, but, of course, not all those he is contriving – is wont to take the form of a many-headed dragon when he specially wants to be noticed, the reason being that a beast of that kind could not (so far as we know) have been created by God.'

'What concerns me, Father Rivadesella, is another kind of metamorphosis, one that seems less logical or, at least, not well suited to the case. According to the report you've just read, among all the figures of witches and warlocks that proliferated last night in the skies over the city, there was one witch more beautiful than the rest, with male genitals, and as she glided through the air she left a silver trail. As I see it, it was more like an angel, and not one of the lesser ones either.'

'We should not forget that the greatest of the angels was Luzbel, and among his attributes was beauty.'

'Does he appear like that before you, as a handsome youth?'

'When keeping his appointments with this humble servant of the Lord, Satan generally chooses more modest shapes. The most dignified of them is that of an elderly gentleman with a self-important moustache. At the other end of the scale comes the dog or the little bird that sits on my lap and speaks to me by signs. Between the gentleman and the bird come all the things Your Excellency might deign to imagine.'

'And how, Father, do you know it is the devil?'

'We have agreed countersigns, and he has explained to me that he assumes one shape or another from mere prudence and so as not to compromise me. Your Excellency should remember that while my relations with the Evil One are known to my superiors in the hierarchy and to the proper authorities, all the way up to Rome, the brethren of my house know nothing about them, even though some bright fellow may have his suspicions. In the same way, Satan hides his relationship with me from his followers. For some reason, yesterday, he not only did not come, but also hid from me his plan to fill the skies over the city with that rabble who are in his service.'

'Very handsome rabble, too, according to the report, and given to all manner of fornication.'

'Was Your Excellency expecting anything else from that class of person?'

'I would have expected that to do it, they would at least have had to lie down. But, as Your Reverence has read for himself, they were doing it right up there in the air, without losing their balance, and prancing about the while. Father Rivadesella, the devil treats his friends so well I'm not surprised he has so many. Does he do any favours for you?'

Father Rivadesella thought for a moment.

'Yes, Your Excellency, but only *gratis et amore*, or so it seems.

I think he needs to open his heart to someone about his worries, and he's chosen me.'

'Because of your sound good sense, perhaps?'

'That might be the reason.'

At that moment a servant came in, went up to the Inquisitor-General, and whispered in his ear.

His Excellency answered: 'Right, show him in.' Then he addressed the Franciscan: 'Your Reverence will presumably have no objection if a Capuchin friar comes in, just for a few minutes?'

'Rivalries have to be put aside in the presence of one who holds such a high office.'

'It's Father Villaescusa.'

'Ah, the senior chaplain of the palace! No small fish!'

'There's nothing small about him, Father Rivadesella. He's on the stout side.'

The servant held the big door open, with its bronze fittings and decoration of pagan (but decently clothed) figures. Father Villaescusa came in, with a series of courtly bows.

'May the Lord be ever with Your Excellency and grant him long years of life!' He put his fingers to his nose. 'So that stink from hell has got as far as this? I am referring, naturally, to that sulphurous smell which has invaded the town and alarmed us all.'

'Up till now my nostrils had not been aware of the plaguey pestilence.'

'I'm in the habit of sensing such things, Reverend Father, as was St Francis of Assisi, my brother in Christ. But everybody knows that this morning a crack opened up in the Calle del Pez and that the stinks of hell came out of it.'

'And what are those stinks of hell, Reverend Father?'

'If we are to believe what tradition tells us, a stink of sulphur, no more and no less.'

'People say it's a healthy smell, and I know places where they use it to fumigate the air and drive off evil spirits. Daemons can't stand it, which is why they blast it out of hell whenever they get a chance. What happened in the Calle del Pez would have resulted from one of those efforts at airing the place.'

'Father Villaescusa: have you made this exceptionally early visit just in order to talk about sulphur?'

'I would not have dared to bother you about such a small matter, Your Excellency, especially when the causes are so publicly known. But something happened last night which justifies my early rising, and my boldness in coming on a Sunday to raise important questions. May I speak in total confidence?'

'Whatever is said and heard in this room is a confessional secret.'

'That puts my mind at rest. The problem can be briefly stated: His Majesty went out whoring last night.'

The Chief Inquisitor gave a start. Father Rivadesella merely smiled.

'What's this you're saying?'

'Simply what everyone already knows in the palace, Excellency, and is becoming known in the town.'

The Inquisitor-General shook his head gravely, like a schoolmaster.

'Someone should start watching the company that lad is keeping.'

'But how can that be done, Excellency, if there are secret ways out of the palace and corrupt servants? Also, we have to reckon with the King's confessor, and this is what I really came about, a doddery, soft-centred eighty-year-old who pardons any sin and issues only the gentlest penances, exceptionally tolerant about the sins of the flesh, no doubt – and may God forgive me if I'm wrong – because he himself once committed plenty of them.'

'He, in this case, I'm sure you mean, is the King, Father Villaescusa?'

The Capuchin felt uncomfortable under the Inquisitor's gaze, and bowed his head.

'Of course, Excellency. I was referring to the King. But I would not wish that to obscure the matter of the confessor.

Your Excellency will recall that his name is Father Pérez de Valdivielso, doubtless a convert from Judaism.'

The Inquisitor took a few moments to think this out.

'The Jews are not characterized by their tolerance. Remember my predecessor Torquemada.'

'The Jews, Excellency, seek to destroy the realms of Spain, and there is no better way than starting with the head of them.'

'With the head of the Jews, Father Villaescusa? I didn't know there was one.' He paused and looked at the friars. 'I did once hear talk of the Great Sanhedrin, but I think that was just a legend.'

'And the Great Turk, is he a legend too?'

The Inquisitor had begun to toy with a pheasant's quill on his writing-desk of embossed silver: a Moorish product, no doubt about it.

'Certainly not. But the danger isn't coming from there.'

'Very true, Excellency. But the danger is coming from England, from France, from the Low Countries, from Germany, and, yes, from Turkey. And who, apart from the Jews, is mobilizing all these against us?'

Father Rivadesella, after saying nothing for a long time, took a hand: 'Against you and against me, Father Villaescusa? I imagine you'll leave the Inquisitor-General out of the conspiracy?'

'When I said "us", I meant the Spains,' said the Capuchin heavily.

The other two exclaimed 'Ah!'

The morning was warming up and even in that room, with its thick walls, it was getting stuffy. Drops of sweat ran down into Father Villaescusa's chin and stayed there, trembling. On Father Rivadesella's face, since he was clean-shaven, they went no lower than his cheeks, where they gathered and began to smell. As for the Inquisitor-General, he was not sweating visibly at all, and so was able to remain more or less at ease, perhaps with his mind reasonably cool too. Father Villaescusa made so bold as to bring out a greenish handkerchief and mop his brow.

'To sum up, Reverend Fathers: first, the city stinks of sulphur, which proves the presence in it of the devil, as was reported to me in due time by a trusted spy in my service. Second, our young King, just twenty years old, went out whoring . . .'

'If you put it like that, Excellency, the affair is a mere anecdote. But – does it have a more important side? Can we forget that the fleet from the Indies is about to arrive, and that there's a major battle being planned in Flanders? If you look at it like that, it's all very different . . .'

The Inquisitor mulled it over, with a rather bored expression on his face. 'It does indeed look different, Father Villaescusa. And what remedy does Your Reverence propose to deal with the threat?'

Father Villaescusa understood plainly for the first time what he had been feeling in the depth of his innermost being: that the future of the world depended on what he now said. He did not hurry his reply, and when he spoke he did not rush his words out but measured them calmly.

'In the first place, Excellency, I propose a meeting of the Supreme Council of the Inquisition this afternoon, augmented by the most reputable theologians of the city. In second place, as a precautionary measure, I propose that the King's confessor should be removed from the palace, he being a known Jew. Finally, that that Marfisa should be thrown into the Holy Office's prison . . .'

'But Marfisa is not Jewish, she's an Old Christian, very faithful in observing the commandments of the Church. I'm sure that right now she is obeying the rule about attending Sunday Mass in her parish.'

'I propose that she should be shut away on suspicion of being possessed by the devil. The King's attitude, ever since he got back to the palace this morning, is highly suspicious. He's wrapped up in himself, as if in total confusion. Who but Marfisa could be responsible for that? Sticking her in some dungeon on a bread-and-water régime seems a useful precautionary measure to me. As for the King's confessor . . .'

'. . . for whom you have expressed great affection,' Father Rivadesella broke in.

'I have no more love for him than I have for any dangerous fellow-creature, Your Reverence.'

'Obviously; but I am not forgetting that Father Valdivielso is a Franciscan.'

'The habit does not make the monk.'

'In that case, who knows?'

It seemed that the two friars were going to renew the ancient and famous dispute between the two differing and warring branches of the followers of St Francis. The Inquisitor-General put a stop to it with an imperious hand.

'Everything that you ask shall be done, Father Villaescusa, and as quickly as possible. For now, you are both called to attend the meeting of the Supreme Council, this very afternoon. Not too early, though, because of the heat. Let's say five o'clock.'

Father Villaescusa bowed his head.

'It seems an irregular time, but I accept.'

'That being so, good-bye.'

When the two friars had made their farewells and could be supposed to have left the Inquisition building, the Inquisitor-General rang his bell gently. A servant appeared.

'Tell my man Diego to come here.'

Diego was more than fifty, with a sanctimonious air and, under that, a cynical smile.

'You know where Marfisa lives. Find her and tell her just three words: go into hiding. See to it double-quick.'

'Yes, Excellency.'

The servant Diego departed, still smiling. The Inquisitor-General, aided by the heavy heat and by pleasant memories of the twenty years he had spent in Rome as a young man dominated by theological passions, gently surrendered himself to the pleasures of taking a nap.

8

They found the King at the door of the secret rooms, known to many as the 'No-entry' area. The big iron key was still in the lock, and the King was leaning against the doorpost, seemingly in ecstasy, which could merely mean that he had a stupid expression. He did not reply to the first questions asked by his valet, and only after he had been shaken with some violence did there cross his face something resembling the gleam on the face of one awakening from sleep. The palace clock was chiming eleven. The valet first whispered to him and then shouted: 'Your Majesty, it's time to go to Mass. The whole court is waiting for you. Your Majesty must change his clothing.'

The King, still with cobwebs over his eyes, allowed himself to be steered along.

'Yes, I must change my clothes. Yes, I must go to Mass with the court. Will the Queen be there?'

The valet led him to the royal rooms along passages that were hardly used at that time of day. Perhaps people avoided them then because they were so much used at night: from them there branched off the secret passageways, the paths along which nocturnal sinfulness glided. Soon the King found himself in front of his large mirror, where the valet was standing with two suits in his hands.

'Will you take the black or the sky-blue, Your Majesty?'

Without really thinking about it, the King replied that he would take the black. After putting it on, he asked for his golden necklace so as to add a lighter touch to the dark monotony. Now they were knocking on the door, asking if the King was ready.

'He'll be ready in a moment!' called the valet, hastening to open the door.

After passing through the small room they entered the large chamber in which the court was waiting. The Chief Minister was prominently on view, as was the Queen, her pretty face wearing a roguish and slightly naughty look, which she now composed so as to accord with the gravity all around her. The King went over to her, greeted her, and offered his arm. His face had not lost its glazed look, and people began to whisper. As they approached the chapel there sounded the trumpetings of the organ and the mellifluous voices of the choir. The procession was now headed by four altar-boys in white and red who swung their censers cleverly, the thin smoke with its suggestion of the Orient arousing a secret sensuality in the courtiers. The chapel, built in the time of the King's grandfather, was simple and imposing. The court could hardly all fit into it: they found places as best they could, each according to his place in the hierarchy. Counts and Viscounts remained standing; Count de la Peña Andrada was there among them, very smart, dressed in English style, positively glowing. Everybody seemed to recognize him, and greeted him with smiles.

Somebody whispered to his neighbour: 'They say he's the one who went out whoring last night with the King.'

'A service the Lord in His glory will reward, no doubt.'

Mass was said by Father Villaescusa. The Papal Nuncio occupied a high seat in the presbytery. It may have been the Nuncio himself who was most nonplussed by the cryptic and generally obscure style of the Capuchin's address: nobody could follow it, least of all the King, his gaze wandering among God knows what shadows, his face still wearing that doltish expression. All that was new was that from time to time he glanced at the Queen, yet it was not precisely at the Queen, but rather at the place where her cleavage ought to be, carefully concealed as it was in Spanish fashion by rich velvets and discreet jewels. The Queen's chief lady-in-waiting touched her from time to time with her elbow: 'Your Majesty, the King is looking at you', but, when the Queen turned her head, the King's gaze had wandered off again towards the misty shapes of his memories.

'He's dying to know if the Queen's got any tits,' a jester commented slyly, receiving as punishment a sharp pinch on his bottom.

'Who shall dare to scrutinize the mysteries of the Divine Will?'

thundered Father Villaescusa. 'Those who attempted it were punished by the Lord with madness and death. He said: "I am what I am", and so that we should not foul the purity of his conscience, He left us His Commandments: "Thou shalt not kill, Thou shalt not fornicate, Thou shalt not commit adultery ..." He was obviously addressing each one of us, but in each one of us human weakness is present. So, to the wonderment of all and so that we should each exercise humility, He left us the mystery of our responsibilities. He addresses each of us, but the responsibility is spread about among all. If the father sins, the whole family pays the price; if the King, his people; if the Pope, the whole of Christendom . . .'

When he spoke of fornication, nobody thought he was being alluded to. When he spoke of adultery, many ladies felt themselves to be more innocent than they seemed. When he assured his listeners that the family paid for the sins of the father, the Chief Minister thought of his wife, there at his side, with her beatific smile and eyes half-closed. Was she thinking, as always, of the pleasures of bed? For a while now the Minister had convinced himself by his own intellectual endeavours, not unmingled with fear, to be sure, that the barrenness of his marriage was owed to his wife being too fond of conjugal fun-and-games, to her cuddling up to him in bed and leading him on, to her rolling her nightdress up more than was strictly necessary. But then, his confessor had told him that none of this was sinful ... What a Mass it was! The Nuncio looked at the preacher and said in an almost audible voice: 'What on earth is this madman babbling about?' The congregation found in Father Villaescusa's words reasons for not torturing their consciences. Count de la Peña Andrada had left the chapel, noiselessly, before the Elevation: he had slipped away like an eel and had been back in his place at the end of Mass, as if nothing had happened. After Mass the Count, when bowing to the King in the assembly room, had been told to put his hat on, to the amazement of the whole court and of the Chief Minister in particular.

However, it was not this surprise that was the subject of comment in the groups gossiping afterwards in the inner court-

yard of San Felipe's, but rather what His Majesty, in a low voice
and with every effort at concealment, had whispered to the
Queen's head lady of the bedchamber, the person closest to her
in terms of protocol: 'Tell Her Majesty that I wish to see her
naked.'

'Your Majesty is mad.'

The lady's face showed something far beyond astonishment,
but she retained enough strength to unburden herself to her
closest friend, as did the latter to the woman standing next to
her, and in this way the King's words went all round the room
until they reached Father Villaescusa, carrying now a charge of
consternation and of foreboding. The friar realized that among
all those people, he alone had the Saviour's righteousness split
between his heart and his head, he alone knew what had to be
done. The Capuchin did not remove any item of his dress: still
wearing his chasuble and all the rest, he stayed at the altar, and
when he stepped down from it, had the Cross and the candles
go before him. In this fashion he perambulated down corridors
and across landings, so that when the King approached the
Queen's apartments and made as if to go in, he stood in the
way. When the King stretched his hand out towards the latch,
the Cross was thrust across the doorway, inclined at an angle to
the vertical, and the King could read in Father Villaescusa's
burning eyes a ban which brooked no appeal.

The King removed his hand from the latch, crossed himself,
and turned to go. To the Chief Minister who was beside him
now, the King confided: 'I wish to see the Queen naked.'

Then he departed, still with his glazed look, but now with a
glint of hope deep in his eyes.

9

Lucretia, alarmed by the loudness of the knocking, rushed to
the door, but on seeing the servant Diego, she burst out
laughing: 'So it's you, you old rascal?'

'I have come to see your mistress, in private and as a matter of urgency.'

Marfisa was in her bath, half-asleep, lulled by the caresses of the warm water. Lucretia's arrival awoke her, and the message about the urgency of Diego's visit gave her a sudden jolt, since it was not customary for messengers from the Inquisitor-General to come so early in the morning.

'It'll be something to do with the heat, and the fact that today is Sunday. Pass me a towel to cover myself with, and show him in.'

When the Inquisitor's messenger saw her, he regretted that even whores, incomprehensibly, should have a sense of shame.

'What's this all about, then?' asked Marfisa.

'The message is very short: go into hiding.'

They looked at each other. They understood. Marfisa said in a whisper: 'Yes. Right. Go now.'

So Diego went, without daring to spy on what might be hidden under the towel: things which Marfisa in her alarm was beginning to display.

She called Lucretia: 'Quick, now. Help me to get dressed. A man's suit. Get the essential things together in a light bag.'

Before Lucretia had come back with her underclothes, Marfisa was already – still naked, but dry – dashing about the bedroom and flinging cupboards open.

She dressed herself, emerging as an elegant youth with fair hair, a lock of which hung over her eyes and concealed them. She tried two hats on, selecting the one with the more ample brim.

'I'm off now. Shut the house up now and get off to where the gossip is. Keep your face covered so that people don't recognize you, listen to what they're saying, and tell them about what happened in this house last night. I don't mean about you and the Count, that won't interest anybody. Spend tonight at a friend's house, or wherever you like, but keep out of the way of the Holy Office fellows: if they don't soon find me, they'll happily take you off and torture you in the hope that you'll tell them where I'm hiding. How can you tell them if you don't know? That's why it would be better if they don't catch you, since you can't confess what you don't know even under torture. Don't forget to go to Mass at the San Plácido convent, because that's where I'll arrange to get news to you. The nine o'clock Mass, eh? Don't get the idea of staying on in bed with some bright spark you fancy or some rich colonial who's paying you well. Now I'm off. You go now as well, as quick as you can. Good-bye.'

Marfisa picked up the bag, pulled the hat down so as to hide her face under the brim, and went out. She made a short detour and set off for the San Plácido convent. She passed people in their Sunday best who were talking about the day's strange events, and found out, thanks to someone who was shouting about it, that His Majesty the King had expressed a wish to see the Queen naked.

'What's it all coming to? If the King doesn't set an example, who on earth is going to?'

When Marfisa got to the convent gate, she asked to see the abbess, who in secular life had been a young lady of the La Cerda family.

'Who should I say wants to see her?' asked the porteress.

'Tell her it's Marfisa. And as you go please take this offering for the poor-box.'

The gold jingled. The porteress greedily stretched out her hand. Then her steps echoed across the floor slabs of the lodge and were lost in corridors and cloisters. Marfisa sat down and waited. It was hot. She took off her hat and fanned herself with it. With her lovely head of hair Marfisa, even dressed as a boy, might have caused more than one who was suppressing unconfessable desires to sin. Now steps could be heard again, of two people and coming the other way. One lot sounded authoritative, the other timid. The porteress opened a small door and asked Marfisa to go in. The porteress then closed the door and locked it securely. The abbess was waiting, smiling.

'I already heard that you announced your coming with a very generous donation.'

'It's one night's earnings, which I offer to Our Lady of the Homeless.'

'What brings you here?'

'I'm looking for a refuge from the constables of the Holy Office.'

'Have they been upsetting you?'

'No, but they soon will.'

'I could send a message to my cousin, the Inquisitor-General, telling him to leave you in peace.'

'It's very good of you to mention it.'

'So . . . ?'

'One nun more, in this convent, will not catch anybody's notice.'

The abbess took her hand.

'Come with me. It's a pity you have to put a habit on – you look very handsome as you are. But I can assure you that I won't demand you cut your hair. Keep out of the chaplain's way, though – he's a very odd fish.'

Still holding her hand, the abbess led Marfisa through a great panelled door, and then along the cool corridors of the convent. Through an occasional window one could glimpse the garden shrubs, and hear the songs of small birds which had sought out their cool shade. The porteress was left wondering what reasons the abbess might have for admitting a handsome young man into the closed convent, but – as she did with so many other things beyond her comprehension – she drove the query from her mind. She felt the heat too, and being on her own in the lodge, felt entitled to roll her habit up a bit and cool her legs in the air coming in through some gap or other.

10

It being so hot, people had left their cloaks at home. They fanned themselves with whatever came to hand, and some appeared with their shirts half undone, putting on view hairy male chests, some dark, some grey. Groups had formed here and there on the steps, in the middle of the courtyard, on the corners, threatening to occupy the very stone slabs of the holy threshold. Clergymen with pointed birettas passed to and fro. The sun kept beating down. The biggest group surrounded Lucretia: she kept her face well hidden, but every now and again lifted a corner of her veil and asked the person nearest her to blow on her perspiring neck. She had already narrated the adventure of her mistress with the King, and was starting to tell about her night with the Count, with generous coverage of the details, but this part seemed not to concern her public so much.

'So there were four mortal sins committed?'

'And one more for luck.'

'Well, four the same night is the limit the theologians set for the excesses of the flesh.'

'How do you know there were only four! You weren't there!'

'But I have it from a trustworthy source.'

'And we know how devoted Marfisa is to the monarchy. Why should she want to show the King up in a bad light? *Quatuor eadem nocte* is a number that would be to anyone's credit.'

'To me, the only believable thing is the business of "one for luck",' said an elderly clergyman with a big nose. 'The rest is just fantasy on Marfisa's part, and it speaks not of any loyalty of hers to our institutions, but of her professional pride. For a woman like her, how could there be any fewer than four capital sins? I can feel some verses coming along . . .'

'Spit 'em out, Don Luis, if you've got them ready in your mind!'

'Just four lines, for the moment, but they might be the start of a ten-line stanza:

> *Con Marfisa en la estacada*
> *entraste tan desquarnido*
> *que su escudo, aunque hendido,*
> *no pudo rajar tu espada . . .'*

'Jolly good, Don Luis! It'll be a rhyme destined for immortality!'

'What the priest has said is a vile slander. The King sinned four times, but during the fifth, he dropped off to sleep. Poor little chap! Whichever way you look at it, the King, though he is King, is still a lad.'

'You shut your mouth, you old procuress. Why should we believe you and not Don Luis? He's a man of some experience.'

'I'd like to know what he'd get up to in bed with Marfisa.'

Don Luis, appealed to in this way, raised his eyebrows and smiled sadly.

'The girl is right. What could I do in bed with Marfisa, except look at her and devise a few metaphors? Maybe a whole sonnet, come to that. But who's the brave fellow who would dare to paint, even in verse, a woman naked?'

Then he made a gesture which alluded to the Inquisition.

It was about that time or maybe a bit later when a new arrival caused a fuss in another group, a fuss so great that it left Lucretia without listeners and, for the moment, Don Luis's *décima* without completion. The new arrival swore on the souls of his deceased relatives that the King, just an hour before, as Mass ended, had said right out loud and without the slightest shame that he wanted to see the Queen naked. 'Did he say "I wish" or "I want"? Because it's not the same,' a voice interjected.

There was a general outburst of laughter, loud, open, and randy, provoked by the varying ways in which each one of those present pictured the King gazing upon the Queen in her birthday suit – by daylight or in the night, in sunlight or in the glow of the oil-lamps. There emerged anew, from thick lips under curly moustaches, remarks about the four sins committed by the King with Marfisa and the much-spoken-of 'one for luck'. There were jokes in very poor taste and disrespectful speculations. Then it all stopped: a starchy man with an ascetic appearance and a dogmatic look stifled the laughter with an imperious 'Gentlemen, behave yourselves!' This, in such a dramatic tone that it had a sudden effect, as though the sun had just set. The group fell silent and everybody stared at the man, severely dressed in black mourning. It was as though into his hand – extended first towards the centre of the knot of people, then placed upon his breast – there had fallen the task of defending the Queen's honour. Yet it was not of her that he spoke when silence gave him the chance to speak.

Instead he said: 'What sort of idiots are you all, gentlemen, to take as a joke something which may bring calamity upon us, and will surely do so unless some remedy is found?' Nobody answered him, except with surprised looks and gestures. He went on: 'It is not only the court protocols that forbid such lunacy: the laws of God and of the Church forbid it too. A man may approach his wife with the aim of procreation, and, if his bodily humours so direct, in order to calm them, but never with disreputable intentions, of which a desire to see one's wife naked would be one.'

Lucretia, finding herself alone, had joined the group.

'The King had a jolly good look at Marfisa, naked, when he woke up this morning, and she was still asleep!'

The man with his hand on his breast turned towards her.

'You ignorant young woman! Looking at a prostitute, who is there for the purpose, is not the same as looking at a woman taken as one's wife with the blessing of the Holy Sacrament. In this case, she may be as French as you like, and we know that Frenchwomen are loose by nature, but on crossing the Pyrenees they absorb our virtues and accept our customs and rules. The body of a wife is sacrosanct. You may touch it, but not look at it.'

'Some fingers have eyes!' Lucretia shamelessly called out. The gentleman with his hand on his breast gave her a look of such searing contempt that the girl, clutching at her veil, dashed away from the group and out of the square, and was lost to view down the Calle Mayor towards the Puerta del Sol.

'That'll be some tart,' one of the group remarked.

Another, an impressive figure, agreed: 'A tart, sure, and I think I know her voice! I could swear that's Marfisa's maid.'

They all turned towards him, and the gentleman with his hand on his breast turned too: they all thought that if somebody knew the maid, he must know the mistress too. The thought made them envious. The man who had last spoken doffed his hat and went off. The group broke up, its members going in different directions. The clergyman who had been addressed as Don Luis sauntered away with a couple of admirers.

'Now about that *décima*, Don Luis: have you finished it?'

'That imbecile with his hand on his breast spoiled my inspiration, but I assure you I'll finish it tonight. What he said was the last straw!'

CHAPTER TWO

I

The cell which the Inquisitor-General occupied in the head-quarters building of the Holy Office did not in its dimensions represent anything like the power of its inhabitant, but it was in proportion to his person: it was large, well shaped, with whitewashed walls and dark beams and furniture blackened by time. To one side was a tiny bedroom which served as a retreat, and though small this was comfortable too. Behind the large table with its velvet cover there hung a picture of Mary Magdalene doing penance in a cave: her hair fell in unlikely abundance but through it you could catch a few glimpses of her golden body. On the other walls, arranged with the most perfect symmetry, were two series of pictures depicting the life and temptations of St Anthony. They formed a balanced set. In the series to the right, by a Flemish hand, the naked women were ugly. In the series to the left, of Italian origin, they were beautiful. An inkstand with twelve pens in it stood on one corner of the table. The bronze and leather stove had embossed decorations on it, the work of Cordobese craftsmen, probably Moors, but these dubious origins did not disturb the Inquisitor's conscience, which had been tempered by the tolerant attitude of the Roman curia. In the far corner, where a window gave light from the left, he had installed a small table with a stove underneath, which he used to take his meals and to warm his legs in the winter, doubting the usefulness (for all its decoration and dignity) of the large stove set in the middle of the room, so imposing that it stopped the visitor in his tracks. The tablecloth was simple, but of good quality; the vessels, of good antique silver; the food, so far as one could see, copious but again simple. The Inquisitor served himself sparingly, what he did not take being returned to the kitchen, where it was devoured by the servant Diego, who liked his food to the point of being unashamedly greedy, and where it made a banquet for the kitchen-boys and other lowly folk. What had been served today was a bowl of soup followed by trout done the Navarrese way, and for the sweet course, a pudding of pastry and egg made for him and for other high-ups by the Santa Clara nuns (that is, Santa Clara la Antigua; the nuns of Santa Clara la Nueva specialized in pickles, but these they did not give away, but sold them, since being the newer they were also the poorer). Be that as it may, the Inquisitor was aware of the tastiness of their cod dishes, pure ecstasy for the palate, attributed to the direct intervention of the angels, though the Inquisitor, better informed, did not make that error.

There was a bird in the room, doubtless a specimen of the migratory flock which had got lost, or perhaps drawn in by the relative cool of the air inside. It flew round and round, blundered into objects here and there, and went out through the same window as it had come in by. The Chief Inquisitor could not have explained why it was he followed its flight with a touch of envy.

The man Diego, sitting on a stool, had pushed aside the already empty soup dish and was getting the bones out of a trout with his horn-handled knife. On the floor beside him he had a big pewter cup full of red wine. The Inquisitor, toying with his pectoral cross, seemed to be lost in contemplation, once the bird had flown out, so Diego felt free to chew away noisily without fearing a rebuke. Then the prelate returned to earth and called him to order.

'Diego, you've interrupted my intended siesta with all those clicks of your tongue and that whirlwind you cause when chewing. I'd be grateful if you'd eat with better manners.'

'Why should it matter, Excellency, now that I've woken you up? A man may be ever so careful when eating, my lord, but he always makes some noise.'

'Ah, now, about noises, Diego: what's being noised abroad in the town today?'

The servant finished chewing the piece of trout which his greasy fingers had lifted to his mouth. He had big hands, and when they poked about in the dish they seemed to cover it.

'A Capuchin friar, one of those from Medinaceli street, sounded the alarm, as if there was a fire, and when people had gathered he spouted a combustacious sermon about how the people will have to pay for the sins of the gentry, or, at least, how the people will have to do public penances in order to counter harm it has not itself done. All this had something to do as well with a boa serpent and a very handsome daemon. I can tell you, Excellency, that the people would have set fire to the palace if the friar had told them to, but he went no further than organizing processions at unusual times, one in each parish, with penitential psalms and himself at the front of some of them carrying a cross. People are really ablaze, and every man-jack can be expected to turn out into the street wrapped in chains. This has got the women all turned on, and when they get home, quite worn out with it all, they're all turned on a different way, and then they have to do another penance.'

'And in the talking-shop . . . ?'

'In the talking-shop, my lord, there were three subjects on the agenda, in the following order. Number One – everyone was talking about Marfisa. Your Excellency knows who I'm referring to. What's she like, what's she like when she's walking, has she got firm knockers or are they starting to droop a bit.'

The bird was fluttering round the garden and calling now and then. It did not seem able to conjure up an image of breasts, either firm or droopy. His Excellency was sorry about this.

'Item Two: if the King had spent the night with her, did this mean that His Majesty had gone up two or three points in the estimation of those present. However, there were some ill-intentioned persons who reduced the royal capacity to zero. Item Three and Last: still about the King, my lord, but this time it was being said that the King had shouted that he wanted to see the Queen naked. On this, my lord, opinion was divided, since some – a few – thought this set a bad example, while others, the majority, thought this was splendid, and that the King should get on with it and stop faffing about. At this, one well set-up man, a colonial rather than a proper gent I should think from his bearing, spoke up more or less as follows: "If the King manages to see the Queen naked, we shall all have a pretext for stripping off our womenfolk, wives or mistresses, and all the females in these realms will strip off, together with the women in the Indies, and all the women in the world will end up naked, if the thing catches on. I think it's really high time, since what with long nightdresses and arguments about lifting them another inch or two, we men are are getting as fed up as they are. The only danger – though this is merely theoretical – would come up if they decide to go out naked into the street, or with dresses so transparent that they're showing it all off, because we all know how keen the women are to reveal their secrets." I am able to assure Your Excellency that in the group in which all this was said there were no priests, or if there was one, he wasn't wearing his religious habit, and wasn't disagreeing with what had been said.'

'The old standards are losing their force, Diego, times are changing, people think differently. I've got nothing against nudity in private, specially in the dark, but taking it out into the street is like taking the spice out of one's meal. I don't know where it's all going to end.'

'Like it's been said around here for a while now, there's a lot of complaisant cuckolds about, and what will happen if it gets any worse?'

'My view exactly, Diego. What's going to become of us? Of your job and mine, for a start.'

'In my case, Excellency, I shan't have long to live, and provided there's enough wine . . .'

He drained the bit left in his glass. The Inquisitor-General closed his eyes and thought about his great old times in Rome. The bird fluttered against the window-panes and then disappeared into the tall cypress tree in the middle of the courtyard.

2

First there was a *Te Deum*, for four voices of both sexes. The organ intervened repeatedly, at times staying well below, as if serving as a support for the melodic pirouettes, at others chasing them in intricate soaring movements, *laudamus, laudamus, laudamus*, until its sound smote the lofty vaulting and was reflected back from it. At other times again the organ shut out the voices from its torrent of noise, and it alone rose and filled the whole space with the wind from its manifold pipes. This was a distinguished piece brought from Rome, where it had been conceived to fill the immensity of the Vatican, but here in the moderate-sized chapel it sounded almost too grand, causing walls to shake and columns to shudder. Then there was the effect of the incense and the heat, so overpowering that one person fainted and had to be carried out, to be revived by brandy and fresh air. This was a tall thin Mercedarian, a specialist in the *De auxiliis* question, which had nothing to do with the agenda for the meeting; but he was too important to be left out of a general consultation such as this. When the *Te Deum* was over the procession formed up in the cloister: two lines of varied habits and the Inquisitor-General at the end, carrying himself stiffly, rather distracted and indifferent to the pages who were holding his train up. They sang the *Veni Creator*, in plainsong, which was easier for them than those Roman polyphonic complexities, though even their plainsong sounded unenthusiastic and some of the voices were rough. It was not a great success, but there it was. Not all those in the procession went on into the meeting-room, which was reserved for those who had places in the Supreme Council, either as full members or as invited theologians. Among these consultants was a Portuguese Jesuit, Father Almeida, still quite young but with a face tanned by Brazilian sunshine. Father Almeida was just passing through Madrid. They had ordered him to go to England as a secret chaplain to a group of people, their former chaplain having been executed. This was equivalent to admitting

that Father Almeida had little time left to live, but he appeared
to be neither preoccupied with his fate nor fired with enthusiasm
about his coming martyrdom. In fact he behaved as though
entirely at ease, unlike his companions, and this despite his
reputation as a wise theologian which his superior proclaimed
in a letter introducing him to the Inquisitor-General, thereby
justifying his presence. Father Almeida stood out somewhat
among the others, since his soutane was topped off by a French-
style collar, and since – when he unbuttoned his dress because
of the heat – there had appeared black stockings and breeches.
However, in a foreigner nobody took exception to this.

After they had all sat down in the council chamber – in
pyramidal order according to their ranks – there was more
praying in Latin, this time without music. The scene resembled
that of the stage in a theatre. At the top was the Inquisitor-
General, the train of his dress extending down among the
inferior ranks and spreading the triple triangle of its tail over
the floor. Below him there came the judges, Father Pérez, Father
Gómez, Father Fernández y Enríquez de Hinestrosa, and so on
up to six in all, some with white habits, others in black, others
again in mixtures of the two. Some were fat and some were thin,
some chubby-cheeked and others hatchet-faced, this one
reserved and that one expansive. Everything known in this
world about God and everything that concerned Him was stored
in the brainboxes of these six; it was they who voted on
decisions, and if there was a tie, the Inquisitor-General gave a
casting vote. The latter had also the privilege of vetoing agree-
ments reached by the others and replacing them by his own
decision, though this rarely happened, mostly because sub-
sequent ill-feeling had to be avoided. Below them were seated
the various experts, on this occasion one from each Order, these
including the Mostensians, the Premonstratensians, and certain
recently founded Orders such as the Society of Jesus of which
Father Almeida was a member. Stealthily there came and went
informers, henchmen, and other low-class persons, until entry
was barred to them a few moments before the oath was taken.
From that time the great council chamber was closed off from

the outside world. Spacious and shadowy, lit by candelabra, it was presided over by a crucifix hung between two lamps: a minimal Christ and lots of candles for so large a room, in which the outstanding figure was that of the Inquisitor-General. So refined, so bored, up there in his presidential chair, almost divine under his cap with its four sharp corners! He generally had a short nap after administering the oath and summing up the agenda items or the facts they were to discuss. This time he added the news that the suspect Marfisa, whom the Holy Office had summoned and ordered to be arrested, had not been found. 'Evidently she was warned and so fled.' Many were sorry to hear it, especially Father Villaescusa, the palace chaplain, who sat sweating among the expert consultants. However, that afternoon the president was unable to take his nap, because the ordinary clergymen were yelling, perhaps because raised voices gave their opinions more weight. Very soon Father Villaescusa stated that he disagreed with the statement that had been made about the events. This had been drawn up in such a way as to give the impression that they had met on account of certain venial sins committed by the King. It was not that anyone had lied – he said nothing of the sort! – but that the events had been related without being interspersed with observations, censures, and condemnations. 'Peccadilloes, nothing! There's been real adultery, real profanation of the Holy Sacrament of marriage!' At this point Father Almeida, the itinerant Jesuit marked down for martyrdom, rose and asked permission to speak.

'I wish to express my doubts whether any adultery has been committed.'

'Is Your Reverence going to deny that the King spent last night in the arms of a prostitute?' demanded Father Villaescusa, as much surprised as he was angered, and in the tone of voice he would have used if Father Almeida had come from another planet and had spoken in some unknown language. 'Or do you deny the truth of what has just been reported to us? This report clearly states that the King spent the night in the arms of that hussy Marfisa.'

'God forbid that I should be so bold!'

'So? Precisely what is Father Almeida's view?'

'I simply doubt whether Their Majesties are married, at least before the Lord.'

Everybody turned to stare at the Portuguese Jesuit. Something like a gale of collective incomprehension blew across their distinguished minds. Even the Inquisitor-General, from his loftily uninvolved height, condescended to inspect him curiously, and it was he who asked: 'What are you saying, Father Almeida?'

The Jesuit remained standing, apparently unaffected by the unanimity of all those disapproving stares. Other voices followed that of the Inquisitor-General: 'Explain! You must explain!'

Father Villaescusa added: 'What you have just said merits a double punishment, one from the Church and another from the State, since what you are attributing to Their Majesties is nothing less than concubinage.'

'Yes: they may not know it, but the Church cannot but be well informed.'

'I insist, Father Almeida, that you should be more explicit,' the president begged in a conciliatory tone.

When Father Almeida asked permission to take his soutane off because of the heat, most of the members of the Supreme Council stared fixedly at him not in a hostile or angry way, but in amazement. Almost all of them felt that the unknown priest should be examined as to the orthodoxy of his beliefs, most considering, without too much of a struggle, that intelligent questioning would suffice without recourse to torture. Among them there were many reputed to be clever interrogators. Father Almeida folded his soutane up carefully and hung it over the back of his chair where his hat already was.

'Reverend colleagues, I am not going to cite the Church Fathers nor Scripture. I merely wish to remind you that moralists and theologians are unanimous in requiring, as a basic condition for marriage, the freedom of the spouses to choose. Now: were our beloved King and Queen free to choose when they married?'

He looked round the gathering. They were listening, but only

Father Villaescusa seemed disposed to answer him: 'Who can doubt it? They were questioned according to the procedures of the ceremony, and both answered "Yes".'

'Could they have said "No"? I beg Your Reverence to consider his reply carefully.'

Father Villaescusa seemed to hesitate a moment. Then he replied: 'I do not understand the question. Father Almeida is too subtle. He doesn't seem to be a Jesuit.'

'Subtle, does Your Reverence say? It all seems very clear to me. Here we have a prince and a princess imbued with princely characters. Here we have two young people who have been taught to obey their parents, parents who are also monarchs. How could they say "No"? Yet their assent was conditioned by their double nature as prince and princess, and as young people. This was not a freely given assent.'

From among the mass of experts there came a tinny voice: 'Perhaps Father Almeida does not realize that he is calling into question the most ancient of our customs, the custom by which the parents decide on the marriages of their offspring, securing as they do so the approval of the Church.'

Father Almeida turned to the speaker, who was an old friar of one of the minor Orders: 'I am not calling anything into question. I am not even offering a judgement. I am merely presenting certain incontrovertible facts to Your Reverences, facts from which in this case, and only in this case, I allow myself to draw some consequences. The rest is a matter for this Holy Office, not for me.'

'Even supposing that Father Almeida is right, the later con-summation of the marriage legalizes and sanctifies it.'

Father Almeida did not have to change his posture or even move his head, for the man who had said this was right opposite him, fully visible in his obvious – though restrained – anger.

'I ask Father Villaescusa to imagine for a few moments what happens when they say to a young man: "Tonight you must go into the Queen's bedroom and do this and that." To the Queen they say: "Tonight the King will come into your room. Let him have his way, because that is your duty."'

'Naturally, yes, Father: that was her duty. Who would dare to doubt it? The wife's duty is to receive her husband in her bed and, as Your Reverence says, to let him have his way.'

'I agree that such was also the duty of the King: but the call of duty leaves no free choice.'

'If we were to follow your doctrine, most marriages would be illegal.'

'That, Reverend Father, is not up to me to say. I content myself with pointing out to Your Reverences that successive approaches by the King to the body of the Queen have been a matter of duty, not of free will.'

'Is Father Almeida not forgetting the obligatory nature of conjugal duty?'

'From whose point of view – the King's or the Queen's?' asked the Jesuit without a pause.

'I understand it as something reciprocal,' said a Dominican member of the Supreme Council from his vantage-point, 'although, naturally, in most cases it's a duty laid upon the wife, who may not always be willing, but even then, she must agree, so as to avoid greater evils.'

'That is not so in our case,' Father Villaescusa replied. 'The King did not go whoring because the Queen spurned him. I have investigated it all. It is some weeks since the King went into the Queen's bedroom. So there has not been any rebuff which might explain (but not justify) infidelity.'

At this point the Inquisitor-General interrupted the discussion with a yawn, a yawn so wide that it nearly dislocated his jaw and so loud that it made Father Almeida's reply inaudible.

'Your Reverences: does it not seem to you that we have debated the first point in the discussion enough? We know that the King went whoring, but Father Almeida, with his great common sense, has sown doubt as to whether our lords the King and Queen are properly married. I have said doubt, not certainty. We will nominate a committee to study the matter and report. That leaves one sin standing, another in the air. What is sure is that the other one concerns the King's confessor, not this Holy Office. Now: I observe that you are feeling hot. I am too. I propose an adjournment while we refresh ourselves with some cooling drinks I have ordered. The session is adjourned for half an hour.'

The members who had been sitting down stood up, fluttering their habits of diverse cuts and colours. The contestants in the dialectical battle waited until the Inquisitor-General had left, after gathering up the long train of his dress. In leaving they took their turn according to rank, which meant that Father Villaescusa and Father Almeida went out together. The drinks were waiting for them out in the cloister.

3

They divided themselves up according to their theological proclivities and their taste for the various drinks: some liked barley-water, some sarsaparilla, and others orgeat. The Inquisitor-General was an exception, preferring cold rosé wine in his Etruscan cup, a valuable piece he had brought from Italy after acquiring it in mysterious and risky deals in which a cardinal of the papal court and a blue-blooded courtesan had played a part, the latter having close connections with the Holy See, from which she had received the title of Princess (and had dragged this through illustrious – or at least rich – beds). His Excellency caressed the exquisite goblet while savouring the wine, both fingers and tongue trembling at the awakening of marvellous memories. From his full height he gazed down at his colleagues: except for Father Enríquez, who had entered his Order only as a consequence of disappointment in love, and Father Almeida, clearly a distinguished man, he viewed the rest as mere rustics stuffed to the eyeballs with Latin texts – some smelly, the rest rough in their manners, sons of the soil, fugitives from the plough. One or two of them would doubtless soon be bishops. God Almighty, please send them to distant lands, where so many Indians remained to be converted even though it be by the lash! Anything rather than going on receiving them in audience one month after another, just to have them put to him problems about rural heresies, or lists of persons suspected of being judaizers or Moors, or names of people given to strange sexual practices. 'Who mightn't be a Jew in this country?' He recalled his great-grandmother, a converted Jewess from Saragossa, who in King Ferdinand's day had used her gold to prop up a most ancient family that claimed to descend from the Goths and was having hard times. The Inquisitor had removed the glove from his left hand – that purple glove of an archbishop *in partibus* – the better to appreciate the coolness of his drink and the delicate sculpture of the glass.

Two Dominicans and two Franciscans had started to discuss the King's sins in the light of the reports that had reached them based on gossip from the people. According to these reports there were three possibilities: four copulations and a failure at the fifth attempt, four copulations achieved, or the failed attempt as the only sinful reality. What was under discussion was not without its complexities: whether the four copulations should be considered as just one sin, or four; whether the failed attempt, in isolation or within a unitary whole, should be considered as a mortal sin in so far as its intention was concerned, or whether in certain circumstances – quite uncertain and hard to investigate, such as whether the intention had been provoked by the female partner or had been a response to a true impulse – it could be defined as merely venial. There was finally the question of whether the female partner, who without a shadow of doubt knew who was sharing her bed and to whom she was offering her collaboration in sin, should or should not be deemed guilty of a crime against the State, and not be treated simply as a habitual sinner against God, in which event she should be transferred to civil jurisdiction and tried according to the criminal law. They were getting going so well in Latin and in Spanish that most of those present had stopped talking in groups and were listening to the friars, with comments for and against what was said, except that is for Father Rivadesella, who was openly laughing at them. Father Almeida was not among them: he was leaning against a pillar and observing how the light was gilding the branches of the trees, and how the flowers were wilting under them. The Inquisitor-General went over to him, smiling.

'It is by no means impossible, Father Almeida, that one fine day you'll be sent for, in a closed coach guarded by outriders, to come and answer the questions which this Holy Office may wish to put to you concerning the orthodoxy of your private doctrine. However, till that happens, I have to tell you that I like you, and I should be pleased if we could have lunch together – just the two of us – before I am obliged to have you arrested. Also, I'm sorry that your journey to England may place your life in danger. I am not familiar with the ways and methods of English justice, but at least I am certain that the power of my hand will not stretch to that country in order to make your tortures more bearable. It would be different here, of course.'

Father Almeida bowed elegantly, more in the French fashion than the Spanish.

'I am most grateful, Your Excellency, for this mark of your consideration, and I in my turn say I welcome both the chance of listening to you and of sharing your table. However, I should warn you that since I have been away from the civilized world for so many years, my manners may not be as refined as your illustrious presence requires.'

'That won't matter, Father. However long you've been away from our world, you will not have lost the good breeding that was taken in with your mother's milk. For my part I should warn you that I keep a very frugal table. The Holy Inquisition is wealthy, but its chief is middling poor. I shall offer you a julienne soup, properly spiced, that's for sure, and a loin of pickled pork that my chef, who's from the north, prepares with consummate skill.'

As he said this he glanced sideways at Father Almeida, who replied calmly: 'That will be perfectly acceptable, my lord. It's all of seven years since I tasted it.'

'So: shall we say noon tomorrow?'

'Won't Your Excellency have to order my arrest before that?'

'I'll try to avoid doing so.'

A servant made his way through the group of friars and

headed for the Inquisitor-General. Asking permission, he went up to him and whispered something. The Inquisitor ordered, 'Bring him in at once,' and politely explained to Father Almeida: 'It's a messenger from the Chief Minister. God knows what His Excellency might want.'

The servant returned immediately with the messenger, a middle-aged gentleman of very dignified appearance and wearing the habit of one of the military Orders. The servant made his way across the room and presented the visitor to the Inquisitor. The man knelt, kissed the hand – or rather, the amethyst ring – that was proffered, and handed over a sealed paper. The Inquisitor opened it, read it, and asked the servant for writing materials. While he waited, he ordered the messenger to stand up, and said confidentially to the Jesuit: 'The people are making a great fuss, going round begging God for mercy on account of the sins of their betters, with an excitable friar at the head of each group. But what appears to have frightened them is the presence of a huge serpent many claim to have seen. Some think it's going to push the city walls down. Others think it's going for the royal palace, but most think it'll attack their own homes. They all know they're sinners.'

'That's the way it goes with public opinion, Your Excellency. There's always someone who creates and manages it, but then each one starts thinking on his own account.'

The manservant now came up with a portable writing-desk which he placed before the Inquisitor. He wrote on the paper, 'Tell the police to lash out right and left. It won't matter if one or two of those friars spend three months in bed with broken legs – it'll give them time to think things over.' Then he passed the paper to Father Almeida.

'I wouldn't like to be in the preachers' shoes.'

'Nor me either.'

The Inquisitor folded the paper, sealed it, and handed it to the messenger, offering his hand in farewell. The man darted between the disputatious priests and went out.

'The blame for all this fuss is Father Villaescusa's. Sometimes passionate faith causes problems with regard to public order.'

'Is Your Excellency referring to Father Villaescusa's faith?'

'You only have to look at him.'

'May God forgive me if I'm wrong, but that priest does not believe in God.'

'What are you saying, Father Almeida?'

'He's one of those who talk, shout, agitate, threaten, all in the name of the purest doctrine, but they never look inside themselves. Have you heard him speak of the Gospels? Does Your Excellency think he has the faintest notion of charity? Father Villaescusa believes in everything that Holy Mother Church believes, but above all else, he believes in the Church, the Church to which he belongs and to which he hands the duty of believing on his behalf. And in the Church, he expects to prosper and, more especially, to be in command. He suspects he'll never get to be Pope, but he doesn't dismiss the notion that he might one day occupy Your Excellency's chair, maybe only to be able to order an auto-da-fé and die next day. It's pretty sure that in that event death would not alarm him and that he would depart from this world pleased at having achieved everything that could be desired in it.'

The Inquisitor paused before replying: 'Father Almeida: for one who has lived so long among savages, you show an excellent knowledge of civilized men.'

'It was precisely because I had gained that knowledge that I chose to live among the Indians. They may not believe in our God, but they truly believe in their gods.'

A little silver bell sounded, announcing the end of the adjournment. They returned to the council chamber in the same order as that in which they had left, and resumed their chairs. The Inquisitor-General asked Padre Villaescusa to speak.

'Reverend Fathers: three questions have brought us together in this solemn gathering. One has already been dealt with: I bow in obedience to the solution proposed, although assured that, in the committee charged with the inquiry, there will be a chance for my voice to be heard again. I pass then to the second matter. His Majesty has declared – with a show of shamelessness tolerable only in royalty – his wish to see the Queen naked.

God's laws prohibit this, and the laws of the realm do also, or, at least, our ancient customs and protocols do so, and have the force of law. What do Your Reverences think?'

Silence answered him. It was eventually broken by Father Almeida, and as some admitted privately to themselves, it had to be he: 'I think that since this is a personal matter, it goes beyond our brief, unless Father Villaescusa can prove the contrary.'

'In order to prove it,' Father Villaescusa replied, with a note of triumph tempered by the certainty with which he was speaking, 'I merely have to state the third question, closely related to the second and also to the first. The Lord God who is all-powerful, He who rewards the good and punishes the evil, is extending over Spain His indignation about the sins of the King. Our nation knows this, and is fearful it may suffer a punishment for evil deeds it did not commit. At this very moment, there is coming up a great battle in the Low Countries which may be decisive for our military power, and the fleet from the Indies is approaching our coast. It is logical that God should punish us by causing us to lose the battle and letting the fleet be attacked and robbed by the English pirates.'

'I see no logic anywhere here.'

A chill could be felt in the bone-marrow of all those present, except in the case of the Inquisitor, who was following the debate with concealed pleasure.

'So you, Father, do not believe that God punishes peoples for the sins of their rulers?'

'I think rather that God punishes peoples for their stupidity and that of their rulers, and helps them when they are not stupid. I beg Your Reverence to consider the state of affairs in the important countries we have as neighbours. England is now a great power, mistress of the seas. The same goes for France, on land. I won't say the same of the Turks, a model of chaotic government. Concerning the late Queen of England, who led her country to prosperity, we have no very favourable reports as to her way of life, and fewer still about her religion. The Cardinal who rules in France is no model of personal virtue either, but he seems intelligent and energetic. So: your theory applies solely to Spain.'

'I find it entirely possible to accept your reply, Father, on condition that God is replaced by the devil.'

'Do you mean that the devil offers greater protection than God, or is God inhibited from acting and the devil benefits?'

'God has not made me party to His secrets and I cannot say how He will carry out His punishment. What I do know, however, is that the devil is patently present in all this, as he is whenever God's plans are thwarted by mankind.'

'By a rotten government, perhaps?'

'Or by a good government, what difference does it make?'

'And does Your Reverence have any sign which betrays the presence, or the intervention, of the devil in the present case?'

Father Villaescusa had been speaking from his seat. Now he rose solemnly: 'This gathering is in itself something more than a sign. The devil caused it to be called, the devil is keeping it going, and the devil is inspiring many of the words that have been spoken and will be spoken here.'

Father Rivadesella spoke up, hardly moving, his tone plainly ironical: 'For the reason we all know, Lucifer last night flew across our skies in the figure of a handsome youth, leaving behind him a trail of silver. There are witnesses.'

'If this is so,' said Father Villaescusa, still with utmost solemnity, 'I propose that this chamber be exorcised at once.'

'Is Your Reverence referring to the space we are occupying, or to the members of the meeting?'

This unexpected and on all scores improper query from the Inquisitor surprised everybody, and Father Villaescusa most of all.

'I was not alluding to anyone in particular, Your Excellency.'

'In that case, we may conclude that the devil's presence is no sort of novelty. The Lord is everywhere, but the devil is always somewhere around.'

'However, at times the Lord is distracted.'

'Then that's very much what I said earlier: the Lord suffers some inhibition – though I find it hard to credit.'

The Inquisitor-General's authoritative tones were heard again: 'I must remind Your Reverences that we are getting away from the subject which brought us here. We had reached the stage of debating whether the King has the right to see the Queen naked, and whether or not this a sin. I beg Your Reverences to come to a decision about this.'

'I assert that he has the right and that it is no sin,' said Father Almeida firmly. 'I assert not only that, but also the propriety of such an act, in order that within the monarchs' marriage, not as monarchs but as Christians, the Grace of the Lord should be apparent.'

Father Villaescusa jumped as though he had been stung by a wasp: 'Did Your Reverence say the Grace of the Lord? Do you think the Grace of the Lord manifests itself in copulation? Or perhaps when one gazes upon those awful appendages women have, called mammaries? Or do you prefer that the gaze should be directed at the woman's back, which is obviously against nature? I allude, of course, to fixing one's eyes on a bottom.'

The Dominican Father Enríquez had dropped off from time to time. At other times he had pricked up his ears, and now and again had smiled. On this occasion he courteously raised his hand: 'I beg the learned and virtuous Father Villaescusa, whenever the discussion is conducted in Spanish, to call things by their names. I mean breasts, not mammaries; arse, not bottom. If my memory serves me, our illustrious poet Father Luis de León, in his version of the *Song of Songs*, translates accurately: "We have a little sister, and she hath no breasts; what shall we do for our sister in the day when she shall be spoken for?".'

He had recited this with evident gusto, and everyone seemed to listen to him with pleasure, except, that is, for Father Villaescusa, who thundered: 'How can Your Reverence dare to quote that, being a Dominican as you are? I remind you that the life and death of that repugnant Jewish convert were in the hands of Dominicans, and that they let him off and deprived the Lord of the pleasure of smelling his scorched flesh.'

'Well, we Augustinians are very proud of him,' the representative of the oldest of the Orders present commented firmly.

'I'm not in the least surprised,' cried Father Villaescusa. 'You're all tainted with heresy!'

There were loud mutterings among the various ranks in the council at the temerity of this choleric Capuchin in his fevered state. The Inquisitor-General acted to calm the row he could see coming: 'Let's leave the dead in peace. I insist that the debate should concentrate on the matter in hand.'

'Then I maintain that the King cannot see the Queen naked without committing a sin. Also that the nation pays for the sins of the rulers.'

'I can tell from the expressions and the whisperings that not everyone agrees with your honourable opinion, Father Villaescusa. Therefore we will nominate members for two further committees to examine the matter in all its complexities. One, to decide whether the King may be allowed to see the Queen without attire which hides, or at least veils, her nakedness. The other, to determine, in the light of the Scriptures and the Church Fathers, whether the nation pays for the sins of the King, taking this to mean not his mistakes as a ruler, but his personal sins. Isn't that right? That harm is caused to states by bad government is so obvious that it's not worth discussing.'

'One needs to know what is understood by "bad government",' said Father Villaescusa.

'Burning Jews, witches, and Moors; burning heretics; curtailing a people's liberties; making men into slaves; exploiting their labours with taxes they can't pay; believing that men are different when God created them equal . . . Do Your Reverences wish me to continue with my list?'

Everybody, this time including the Inquisitor-General, had listened to Father Almeida in utter amazement. A collective whisper ran round the room: 'We've just got to bring this Jesuit to heel.' The first protest was about to be voiced when the servant came in and whispered in the president's ear.

'One moment, gentlemen. We have an unexpected visitor.' To the servant he said: 'Show him in.'

The servant quite overdid the bowing and scraping to right and to left. Hardly had he gone out than the door opened again and there, framed in its space, appeared Count de la Peña Andrada. He stood there, doffed his hat, and bowed to the company in the most orthodox fashion.

'Please come forward, Count.'

He did so, but not before repeating his bow, this time a triple one, as though the company consisted of royalty, brushing the red carpet with the feather in his hat. On coming forward and passing in front of the crucifix with its lamps, he repeated the bow with even greater elegance. He then drew himself up and faced the Inquisitor.

'I can imagine that with the tensions of the debates, Your Excellency has not noticed that the wicks of the candles have grown very long, and that the flames are guttering. When the flickering light falls upon the Lord's face, it appears to darken. With Your Excellency's permission, I should like to trim the wicks.'

Hardly had the prelate time to reply, in a tone of some surprise, 'By all means do so if you wish,' than the Count drew his sword and with a lightning-quick slash chopped off the candle on the right. Those present scarcely had time to express their astonishment when a voice was heard to whisper, 'He dares to unsheath his blade before the Crucified Christ!' Already the Count had trimmed the candle on the left with another slash: the two candles matched perfectly in height and in brilliance, with no more than the slightest flickering. The Count laid his sword at the foot of the crucifix.

'I am yours to command, gentlemen.'

He stayed firmly positioned facing the gathering, on the precise spot where witnesses stood when they appeared to give evidence.

The Inquisitor asked him: 'Why has Your Excellency come?'

'The whole city is talking about what is being debated here, and I thought it polite to offer my testimony, which I shall do with pleasure, but not before greeting an old friend I see is present here.'

Without asking permission, he went over to the ranks of the consultants and held out his hand to Father Almeida.

'It's a while since we met, Father.'

'You're right, it's been a long time.'

While they were shaking hands, Father Rivadesella studied them, and it seemed to him that they had a certain likeness, although in more important ways they differed. He searched his memory, but the only thing he came up with was a cockerel, not oversized, but yet somewhat larger than they usually are, larger too than capons get; a cockerel that had something odd about him, maybe his crest. Meanwhile the Inquisitor had asked where their acquaintance had begun.

'Father Almeida several times provided the ships in my squadron with fresh water and foodstuffs, over on the coasts of Brazil, when he was exercising his ministry there.'

'And what was Your Excellency doing in those remote parts?'

'I was serving the King with my ships, my lord. It was dangerous work: at times our only recourse was sheer heroism. But I can assure you that in my reports there was mention only of the heroism of my men, who are under no obligation to be heroes, but who can be as if it were the most natural thing in the world. They took no pride in their daring, but were glad to have a rest from it.'

'So, you're a pirate?' asked Father Villaescusa, unable to contain himself.

'Not exactly, Father. I'm a privateer, and I sail with the royal warrant.'

'That being so, why are you not out protecting our fleet as it sails towards Cadiz under threat from the English?'

'I was not informed about it, nor was I invited to sail with them. My squadron is resting now at its base, over there in a northern harbour which I am sure Your Reverences have never heard of. However, Father Almeida knows it. Father Almeida is Portuguese, and knows more about seafaring matters than Your Worships do.'

'I was born in Rivadesella, and my father was a seaman. I went to sea a bit, as a child. Of course, it wasn't in a big ship, just in a rowing-boat.'

'And you've never forgotten it, have you? The sea is like a girl you were in love with, shy and unattainable, the one who stays on in your heart. I could tell you the story of one such, a dark girl from Honolulu, who refused to come with me and share my command.'

Father Villaescusa, visibly restless, advanced a step towards the Count. 'I hope your Lordship will understand that such a comparison and such a tale is out of place here, where we are all celibate and probably chaste too. I hope also that your presence in this Holy Office is not owed to your wish to tell us about the charms of the sea and the seafaring life. As Your Lordship can see, we're serious people here.'

When he mentioned chastity, several heads had turned towards the Capuchin: some angrily, others, with ironical expressions. The Count merely smiled, but not too openly.

'But would Your Honour be thinking that we're not serious about the sea? Do you know what a tornado is, and how a ship may defend itself against the unstoppable fury of its wind?'

The Inquisitor-General resolved to impose some order.

'I admit I'd like to hear from the lips of the Count how ships escape from the dangers of wind and water, since I too am a landlubber, and the journey I undertook to Italy in my youth was not in a galley but on muleback. But I agree with Father Villaescusa that this is not the right place for all that. I agree too that the Count could not have come here to relate his adventures to us.'

'Obviously, Excellency, I have come in order to answer questions, but so far nobody has put to me certain questions I was expecting. I am at your disposal to answer them.'

'Have I your permission to make a start, Your Excellency?' Father Villaescusa asked the Inquisitor. The latter gave it.

Sweat was running down Father Villaescusa's cheeks, making his forehead and his nearly bald tonsured pate shine. He mopped his head with his colourful handkerchief, the one which from the start had seemed vulgar to the Dominican Father Enríquez, but which had seemed perfectly natural when used by such an ostentatious Old Christian as Father Villaescusa. The Count – his own face free of sweat – looked at him expectantly. The

Capuchin's handkerchief stank: the Count drew his own from his sleeve, a white lacy one, and offered it to him. Father Villaescusa mopped his brow with it, returned it, and asked: 'Why doesn't Your Lordship sweat?'

The Count laughed. 'It depends on the bodily humours, Father. Ours must be different. But sea breezes dry the skin and harden it. Maybe that's the reason.'

'Whatever the reason, it doesn't matter to me. But I have another more delicate question to put to you. Is it the fact that – as gossip has it – you accompanied the King last night on a certain enterprise?'

'That is so, Father. I went with him to the house of one Marfisa, a famous courtesan of whom those present may have heard tell. They say she is the most beautiful woman in the city, and that in her clientèle there figure great lords of high public standing. If I were not where I am, I would venture to add that she is credited with having relations with certain cardinals, but we all know how evil-minded people gossip. She's an expensive woman: ten golden ducats per night, and she doesn't generally offer discounts, although as you can imagine she sometimes yields to a whim. That does happen with women of that profession, though it's not to be recommended. If Your Reverence wishes to know why, I could explain it to you.'

The Capuchin gestured in disgust.

'I know all I need to know, my good sir.'

'Still, it's as well to know all the details.'

'Was a whim involved in this business with the King?'

'I can assure you it was not, Father. I had to pay the ten ducats myself. The King did not have enough cash on him. All he had was a golden half-ducat in a pocket that was usually empty! By the way, someone should think about changing some details in the protocol. Half a ducat for that type of services may have been all right in the days of the Great Duke of Burgundy, but prices have changed a lot since those times.'

'Services for which the King shouldn't have paid a single brass farthing!' a distant voice angrily exclaimed. The Inquisitor smiled.

Father Villaescusa begged the meeting not to stray from the business in hand.

'Your Reverences: we find ourselves faced with a clear case of pimping. It's not up to us, but to the secular courts, to judge it. Let's hand his Lordship the Count over to them: he'll be sentenced to several years in the galleys.'

'I would serve them willingly if I had committed any crime, since being chained to a bench in a galley is better than being in some dungeon of a prison as they are now. But I do not accept that accusation of pimping.'

'I think it's perfectly plain,' said Father Villaescusa, 'and moreover, Your Lordship has confessed.'

'No, Father. I didn't confess, I told the story, but I didn't tell it all. What happened was the following. I was in a room in the palace . . .'

'And what was Your Excellency doing in a room in the palace, since it seems you are properly the commander of a squadron?'

'I had come to hand over to the Treasury the fifth part of my prize-money, which is owed to the King. A whole bag of ducats, or to be more precise, in this case, of pounds sterling, since that's what English money is called. The King noticed me, approached me, asked who I was and what I was doing there, and I told him. Then he asked: "Well, if you're not from these parts, I suppose you won't know where a certain Marfisa lives. I'd like to spend the night with her." I replied: "No, I don't know, my lord, but I can find out." Then the King surveyed the grandees, the noblemen, all the courtiers who were standing about in the hall in groups, chatting and laughing, that is those that weren't voicing complaints or just getting plain bored. "These people all know." "Then it won't take me long to find out." I left the King's side and looked around, and soon came back with the precise address. Is there any crime in that? The King said: "Many thanks for the information." I asked: "But is Your Majesty proposing to go alone to such a well-frequented place? I've heard that it's hardly very safe to go about the city by night." "But if any of these people were to accompany me, the whole world would know about it tomorrow." 'So I said:

"Nobody knows me here, my lord, and I have a coach and a sword which has been well tried-out in tougher battles than any night-time assault in the street. I offer myself to be your companion." "So: wait for me tonight in your coach at the south-east corner of the palace. I'll be dressed in black, but I'm sure you'll recognize me despite the darkness." "Have no fear, Your Majesty. I would know you in the very pit of hell." That was all, gentlemen. I consider that what I did was provide protection for the King's person.'

'And while the King was fornicating, what was Your Lordship doing?'

'Sleeping, Father, have no doubts about that. I was sleeping on an uncomfortable armchair, with my collar undone, my belt slackened, and my boots beside my feet. That is, until the King woke me up. He was already dressed, and told me we should go. It is the case that he had a glazed look. I asked him if he was all right. He answered that he'd seen a woman naked for the first time, and had not imagined it could be anything like that, so unexpected and so lovely . . . which is pretty odd in a man aged twenty and one who is, moreover, married.'

'Don't forget, my lord, that he is married to a queen.'

'So I understand, although I don't know her. I have heard reports about her father. He had few scruples when it came to women, so it shouldn't surprise the Queen when her husband seeks solace in other beds.'

'Is Your Lordship justifying it?'

'No, Father. I am merely explaining it.'

'There are some explanations which imply an argument in favour.'

'Mine had no aspirations to that.'

Father Enríquez, who was getting bored with the discussion, asked permission to speak. When this was granted, he shot at Count de la Peña Andrada: 'And does Your Lordship think that this whim of the King's – to see the Queen naked – bears some relation to what you've been telling us?'

'I believe, Your Reverence, that here we have cause and effect. A logical effect. A necessary effect, as well. Young men who go about in the world should be informed, not innocent. What else can one expect of a husband than that he should know what his wife's body is like?'

Father Villaescusa intervened, fearful that Father Enríquez, with his reputation for tolerance, might steal his leading role: 'My lord: have you seen many naked women? Did you enjoy looking at them?'

'Reverend Father, more than half the women in the world go about unclothed. Not just in the south seas, where you can't tell if they're women or mermaids, but also in other regions. You just ask Father Almeida.'

Father Almeida took the challenge up with all due seriousness.

'The Count is right. The women in the tribes I baptized went about naked, and I suppose they still do.'

Father Villaescusa turned on him angrily: 'Didn't you, Father, force them to dress? Wasn't that the prime objective of your ministry?'

'I, Father, taught them that the Son of God had died for all men, including them, and that He is waiting for them in paradise.'

'Paradise, for naked people?'

'We do not know how people who have deserved it live in paradise, but I suspect they haven't taken their clothes with them.'

It was getting dark. In the wan light of the candles, all the faces seemed ghostly. But nobody believed in ghosts. Least of all the Jesuit and the Count.

CHAPTER THREE

I

Father Villaescusa entered the Chief Minister's office utterly worn out: partly because of the mental anguish suffered that afternoon, partly on account of the heat, which had not lessened at sunset but persisted heavy as lead. He had shuffled along the street and had stopped every few steps to wipe the sweat with his big green handkerchief. When he got in through the door reserved for secret visitors, he collapsed into an armchair and asked for water and for something to fan himself with. Someone passed him at once a file containing letters patent of nobility, from among those heaped up on the Minister's desk, but he had to wait for the water. The Minister made the delay bearable by serving a glass of brandy, from the bottle he used himself in moments of depression, as when he despaired of ever having a son or when bad news pouring in from the provinces made his head spin and weighed on his heart. The arrival of the water seemed to unstick Father Villaescusa's tongue from the roof of his mouth in a way that the brandy had not managed to do, perhaps for some moral reason. He sighed long and deep.

'Things are going badly, Your Excellency,' he said to the Minister.

The Minister's answer was a question: 'Which things do you mean?' – since at that moment there were scores of worries buzzing about in his head, and any of them might be "things".

'I allude, Excellency, to the sins of the King. However, thinking it over, there's something much more serious: the Holy Office of the Inquisition is in powerless hands, not from weakness, but from laziness. Everybody is immensely learned, but nobody believes in anything, not even in their own knowledge.

Can Your Excellency imagine what was the outcome of a whole afternoon's discussion? The setting-up of four committees charged to discover whether, in the light of doctrine, Their Majesties are really married; whether or not the carryings-on of our lord the King were adulterous; whether or not it would be a sin for the King to see the Queen naked; and finally – prepare for the shock, your Excellency! – whether the sins of the monarch have an influence or not on the triumphs or disasters of these realms. In these days there are no safe doctrines left. It's enough to drive one mad.'

The Minister, who had been standing by his desk, took a few steps in silence over to the open window, breathed in the air coming up from the Campo del Moro, and rested his gaze for a few moments on the horizon, where a red glow marked the place where the sun had just set. Then he walked back to the desk.

'And can Your Reverence propose any remedy?'

'In the long term, Excellency, replace the Inquisitor-General, if it should turn out that someone appears disposed to make the sacrifice – that is, given the chaos that awaits him! In the short term, the remedy is one that you, Excellency, and I have to agree on right now.'

'And your remedy is . . . ?'

'Stopping the King from seeing the Queen naked. Last night's sins are quite sufficient to endanger the monarchy, and with the monarchy, the whole of Christendom. If we add to those sins the one involved in the monstrous contemplation of nakedness, prohibited by both human and divine laws, I dare not imagine what might become of us.'

'By "us", does Your Reverence mean yourself and me?'

'I refer, as you may well understand, to the future of the sole country in the world which is defending the doctrine of God and of His Holy Church.'

'You use very large words.'

'Those appropriate to the case.'

The Minister again traversed the distance between his huge overburdened desk and the window. It seemed that his gaze slipped across the empty skies and was lost along the pink line of the horizon. The fact was that he was trying to banish from his mind the memory of his wife, naked on the bed and begging him to undress too.

'And you say that the Inquisitor-General is a weak man?'

'It's the whole Holy Office, Excellency! It has stopped being the firm right hand of the Lord, and is now a sort of salon where the members chat in Spanish and nobody expresses strong views about the matters under discussion. If they think you're tired they give you a cooling drink, and nobody bothers to think about turning divine wrath away!'

'A cool drink, now, on afternoons as hot as this, seems a good idea to me. Right now I could do with a bit of brandy in iced water. I've had a very busy afternoon, even though it's Sunday. Did you know that we've had no recent news about the fleet? And that we don't know anything about how the fighting in Flanders is going? Also, the Genoese bankers are pressing us, and if the fleet is delayed, or is attacked by pirates, we shan't have enough money to buy the King his meals.'

The Capuchin crossed himself ostentatiously, using the big crucifix which hung from his rosary.

'Praise be to God! May He forgive me if I have spoken with excess of pride, but it wouldn't do the King – and come to that, the whole court – any harm to have a week fasting, and even doing penance, with hair shirts and a few lashes.'

'You may well be right, Father, but what will they think of us in all the foreign courts? It's just the decorum of the monarchy I have in mind . . .'

A small bird shot in through the open window. Exhausted, it collapsed on Father Villaescusa's lap, limply moving its wings and gasping for air through its open beak.

'It's dying of thirst,' explained the priest.

The Minister remarked: 'We've forgotten the water and the grappa. It's made from my vineyards in Loeches, and it's really good stuff.'

The priest stroked the bird's back and helped it to move its wings. The Minister called his servant and a jar of iced water was brought, a big silver jar, and two glasses. The bird drank greedily, tried a couple of flights round the room, and went out through the window. Father Villaescusa – his glass in his hand, the water discoloured by the jet of liquor – watched it go, murmuring thoughts about the freedom and carefree life birds enjoy, of which Christ had spoken. The Minister's glass rested on a corner of the table, half-empty already, and with its contents somewhat more discoloured than the priest's.

'Now that we've wetted our whistles, we might continue our discussion of the case.'

'Which one, Excellency? I mean the cases, not the whistles.'

'I see just the one, or rather, many facets which we can reduce to one case. Are you advising me to get the Nuncio to come so that I can ask him to replace the Inquisitor-General?'

The priest put his hands to his head, without setting his glass down.

'Your Excellency should do nothing so foolish! The Nuncio is Italian, and his mansion has a bad reputation in the city. Moreover, the Inquisitor-General spent his youth in Italy, and there suffered the contagion of easy-going Roman ways. I would send a special courier to our ambassador with instructions to attend to the matter personally and in secret. We would have to send a true account of events, not drawn up by some backroom lawyer, nor, worse, by some grubby pen-pusher, however elegant his hand, because in that event the result would be a gloss upon words of mine as heard by Your Excellency and then transmitted to a secretary and on again to a scribe. What would be left of my report?'

'So Your Reverence is suggesting that he should set down the account himself?'

'The main gist of it, my lord, at least, yes. I am a witness with a good memory.'

'I may add, dear Father Villaescusa, that to the account of the events there should be added the proposal that you be nominated for the post.'

Father Villaescusa fell on his knees. He could not manage to control an outburst of feeling, part amazed, part joyful.

'Excellency! My merits do not warrant that! I don't know if in my humbleness I can accept.'

'If it comes from the Holy See, signed and sealed by the Pope, you'd have no option. But that will take several months … Allow for two journeys by the couriers, and how long for the secret negotiations? I share Your Reverence's feeling that we must get out of this imbroglio with all speed. How do you propose we should do this?'

Father Villaescusa had now stood up, with a less than humble expression, indeed with the look of a man marked out as Chief Inquisitor. He replied in almost booming tones: 'Excellency, palace affairs are in your hands. For my part I shall attend to spiritual ones, if I am authorized to do so.'

'You have that authorization.'

From that moment Father Villaescusa gave free rein to the imaginings already forming in his mind, already hastening towards their practical realization. He could not avoid seeing himself as a huge octopus whose tentacles embraced the Chief Minister and the King, the monarchy and the whole world. It occurred to him that such an image came from the devil, but he accepted it all the same, and saw himself as an octopus bedecked in a cardinal's purple, and with an Inquisitor-General's powers.

2

Mademoiselle Colette – who looked rather less than her forty-odd years, and had a reputation in certain palace circles for real sportiveness, high frolicsomeness, in bed – was about to leave when the Queen spotted her in the mirror and called to her. The Queen was in her boudoir, full of French objects, frivolous and cheerful, things that none of her Spanish ladies-in-waiting approved of because they were in their view not proper: the mirror with a silver frame, the chest of drawers with naked Cupids painted on it, and most of all, the cupboard on whose doors Adam and Eve displayed themselves without figleaves … in fact, with everything on display. Not even the King had ever

been so shameless, since he, nearly every day, habitually dressed
in the severest black.

'Come here,' said the Queen to her personal maid, the maid
who had accompanied her from Paris after serving her there for
a number of years. 'Come close, Colette, and let's talk very
quietly.'

'Nobody among those who are around understands
French . . .'

'Maybe . . . but in royal palaces there are always more
informers than there are rats.'

'As Your Majesty wishes.'

'You may sit as well, on that chair, right at my side. As close
as possible.'

Colette was highly delighted: 'Thank you, Your Majesty.'

'Now: tell me what all the world is talking about.'

'I can't tell you anything Your Majesty does not already
know. I already told you that the King is going around looking
pretty gloomy.'

The Queen sighed, and put the silver comb with which she
had been doing her hair down on the dressing-table that had
belonged to her mother.

'That poor husband of mine, such ideas he gets! If you were
me, what would you do?'

'Strip off in bed, without a moment's hesitation.'

'Have you ever done that?'

'Ever since I knew two and two make four, Your Majesty,
when the occasion demanded it, I've stripped off, yes. My
mother taught me that things should be done properly. That is
why I serve Your Majesty in the perfect way I do.'

'I've no complaint about you, Colette, as I've often told you.
But . . . this business of stripping off in bed . . . do you know if
the Queen of France does it?'

'The late King, your father – God rest his soul – never did it
any other way.'

'Do you know this because they told you so, or because you
saw it for yourself? You were still very small when my father
the King died . . .'

'Not all that small, my lady. Your father the King – may he rest in peace, either as a Protestant or as a Catholic – whenever he caught me alone, which was quite often, used to strip me down so that the only thing I had left on was my shoes, since I never wore stockings. Not even in a court as icy as this one sometimes is.'

'Doesn't that make you out to be entirely shameless, Colette?'

'What else would you expect me to be, living always in the palace? Decency doesn't exactly thrive along these corridors.'

The Queen stared at her for a moment, then turned her head towards the mirror, lit by two candelabra overloaded with lights.

'Do you think I look all right, Colette?'

'Yes, fine, more than ever.'

'Do you think the King will fancy me just as I am, without any make-up?'

'Your Majesty should give up rouge for always, as I've often told you.'

The Queen studied her eyes, multiplied several times over by the lights in the mirror.

'So you think I should await the King naked in my bed?'

Colette cried out in alarm: 'Never, never do that, Your Majesty! Let him take the trouble to undress you.'

'And I'm not to be too coy about it?'

'Just a bit coy if necessary, but don't overdo it.'

The Queen thought for a moment, still meeting the maid's eyes: 'Colette, as soon as I sit down to supper with those old cows who keep me company, you go and look for the King, and tell him I shall expect him at eleven. Does that seem the right time to you, eleven? At that time of night the corridors are usually empty.'

Colette rose and curtsied.

'Your Majesty, for a lovers' tryst any time is a good one.'

She stepped back, curtsied again, and went out. The Queen sat on, trying out the various images the mirror reflected, and resolving to adopt the one she liked best.

3

The dowager Duchess of the Maestrazgo, chief lady-in-waiting to the Queen, had held the same office under her predecessor, and the fact that she was able to continue in the post when the new Queen arrived from France was owed to her profound knowledge of palace affairs. It is certain that it had not been within her power to help her cousin into the position of Chief Minister, but the relationship had been no drawback either, since they got on well, and had played together as children. Indeed, the first female thighs seen by the boy who was to become an all-powerful man had probably been hers, at an age when he did not know what features might distinguish them from male ones. The widowed Duchess had absolute control over the palace's feminine world, and between her and her cousin there was an unspoken agreement that she enjoyed this control by a further delegation of authority, secrets being exchanged and benefits shared. The Duchess was only a year older than the Minister, and when she was widowed, she would without a doubt have married him had he not been in such a hurry to marry Lady Barbara, which was not for any honourable reason of family or personal advancement, but merely because he found her attractive and wanted to go to bed with her. In spite of all this, the widowed Duchess bore her cousin's wife no ill-will, and was genuinely sorry that heaven had not granted them any offspring. 'I had only two years married, but I brought two daughters into the world, two raggedy girls it's impossible to bring up decently. If I'd been married to my cousin, I'd have produced a dozen at least, and even if some of them had died, there would still have been a surplus big enough to satisfy my poor cousin's paternal yearnings. On the other hand, I would have ruled in my house, and in the Loeches mansion, and in two or three other spots, but not in the royal palace.' When she received the Minister's request to go his office as soon as her duties allowed, she hurried along there. She looked attractive, that hot Sunday afternoon, in a light dress with a cleavage somewhat more generous than her confessor allowed her (though her confessor already set limits for the cleavage in the knowledge that they would be disregarded).

The Chief Minister sat lost in thought, and took a few moments to realize that his cousin had come in. She was waiting with a smile, maybe laughing at him for taking affairs of state and matters concerning Their Majesties so very seriously.

'You know why I asked you to come?'

'I can imagine.'

'You'll know all about this little game of the King's.'

'The whole palace knows about it, the whole city, and soon every part of the kingdom will know.'

'And what do you think about it?'

'That you're making what you call the King's little game out to be much too important. What I think is that if husband and wife want to sleep naked in the same bed, it shouldn't go outside the bedroom walls.'

'Well, as you see, it has gone outside. Protocol is all against it, and now the priests want to have their say.'

'The protocol is out of date, and as for priests, you mustn't let them get too uppity.'

'But they have got uppity.'

The Duchess had sat down in an armchair by the window, with her back to the Minister, all spread out, with her skirts rolled up so that her burning legs could get some air. Even so, she spoke in a tired voice and fanned her face with her hand. The Minister offered her a cool drink, and she accepted. He brought her a glass of iced water with a dash of brandy in it, and she, on hearing his approach, quickly drew her skirts down. She took a couple of sips and asked: 'Did you send for me just to say all that, or do you want something from me?'

'I do want something, yes. I want you to prevent the King sleeping with the Queen, at least until we have news of the fleet and the war in Flanders.'

The Duchess handed him back the empty glass.

'Fill this up again for me, and double the measure of brandy.

What on earth has the King's whim to do with the fleet and with
the war in Flanders?'

'For the fleet to reach Cadiz safely, and for us to win or lose
in Flanders, it all depends on the King's sins.'

The Duchess gave a great laugh: 'I can never reason out why
the country is so full of idiots who believe in such things.'

'It's what the theologians think.'

'I'd say it again even if the Queen of the Fairies thinks the
same.'

'I can't go against the dictates of the Church.'

'It's always possible to find one set of priests who think the
opposite of another group.'

The Minister drew up a stool and sat on it in front of his
cousin, with his back to the window.

'The pity of it is that that has already happened, and it's got
us bogged down.'

'Well now, I, in your position, would look for a third group
of priests. And before consulting them I'd give them a right good
meal.'

'You make it all sound very easy, but things are more
complicated than you think.'

'So that's the reason, that they're complicated, why you want
to stop those two young people from having their fun in the
nude?'

'Did you do it that way with your husband?'

The Duchess took a long drink from her glass before replying.
The drink was not so cold now, but the brandy put life into her
tired limbs.

'In the first place, the Duke, when we got married, was not so
young, and the rheumatism he acquired during his life at sea
didn't allow him to move freely. In the second place, the galleys
he commanded and the Turks and all that mattered more to him
than I did. When we got married, the moment we were alone,
he grabbed me in a corner and left me pregnant. With that, he
considered he had done his duty, and went back to his galleys.
Then when I went to meet him in Valencia, he grabbed me
again, this time in a corner of his admiral's cabin, and there I

was pregnant once more. As his ship sailed out of Valencia, the Turks were waiting for him, and a cannon-ball shattered the bow and sank his galley. He couldn't swim, and he was drowned. I should add that, fond as he was of salt water, he was not overfond of fresh water and soap. He stank like a peasant, poor devil, and if he smelled like that when dressed, what would he have been like naked? And then, as I've been telling you, he was in such a hurry that on neither occasion did he give me time to hint that he should strip off.'

'Nevertheless, you owe him a lot for your rise in the world.'

'That I have never denied. The truth is I do owe him a lot, poor devil, but only because he died. If he'd been able to swim . . .'

The sky had darkened, and all the Duchess could see of her cousin was a shadowy silhouette. Suddenly the Minister stood up. She heard the sound of flint and tinder, and a flickering yellowish glow appeared.

'Do you find it a bit too cool now with the window open?'

'Shut it if you like.'

The Minister shut it. The Duchess stood up, moved the chair over to the table, and sat down again.

'Right, let's get back to business.'

'The business being . . . ?'

'You're to use every means to prevent the King going to the Queen tonight. I will use my own means for the same.'

She stood up.

'That's right. It's always best to be on the safe side.'

'What precisely will you do?'

'There's a passage with three doors, leading from one bedroom to the other. By tradition, locking each of those doors means something different. It'll be the first time all three have been locked, so far as I know.'

The Minister stood up.

'Right. I'll take charge of the other entrances. And I'll keep you informed.'

'And tomorrow, when the Queen questions me?'

'That's up to you. You'll be able to invent some lie.'

'I suppose so. It's what I do all day long.'

'Does that include lying to me?'

The Duchess went up to the Minister and gave him a kiss on the cheek.

'I've never made an exception of you in the palace.'

The Minister, left alone, remained seated at his desk, with the impression that this kiss was the first chaste one his cousin had given in her life.

4

Father Valdivielso's cell was a wretched little room situated remotely near the north-western tower of the palace, assigned to him because it was so cold that it could be hoped he would at last die of it. The fact was that Father Valdivielso had already lived far too long, with all of eighty years weighing him down, as did the burden of a distant but distinguished military past in all the wars of the Empire fought under Philip II, Philip the Great. Nobody knew why he had gone into the priesthood, but it was known that when he was chosen to be the royal confessor, the Order to which he belonged had got rid of him with the cheerful approval of its officers, since a man who had bedded Italian, Flemish, French and (it was said) Turkish girls could not serve as an example to men who had only Spanish girls – and these extremely prudish ones – at their disposal. Father Fernán de Valdivielso had been the director of the King's conscience for some years now. He operated in the permissive spirit of the old soldier who knew all about varieties of behaviour and of consciences, and who, each time an awkward problem came up before him, rather than consult his books or living authorities about it, relied on his memories. There were those who, hoping the King would continue along the path of perdition he was set upon, wished him long life, but others, aspiring to take control of the King's conscience, wished him an early death and used all legal means to see that this happened. That was why they had moved him from a sunny cell overlooking the parade-ground to his present cell, a freezing pigsty never touched by the sun. Father Valdivielso managed as best he could, with blankets and stoves. Being so old he went from his bed to his armchair and back again, making no other journeys except those required by nature, in the knowledge that on one of these trips his hour would strike and he'd be stretched out there in the passageway. The King was fond of the old captain, and many were the mornings when instead of telling the priest his sins he would listen to the old man's tales of battles long ago when the royal armies fought with the certainty of winning. 'What great times those were!' None the less, Father Valdivielso had come to the conclusion that war was a barbarous business, and that disembowelling Huguenots was a disagreeable thing to do, however much the Church went on blessing it. The fact was that Father Valdivielso, if he had not taken refuge in that slum in the north-western tower, would have ended up burned at the stake.

When the King knocked at his door that hot Sunday afternoon, Father Valdivielso was dozing, not at all incommoded by the heat which was good for his old bones. He didn't hear the gentle tapping of the royal knuckles, and the King pushed the door open and put his dishevelled head in. Round his neck he was wearing his little chain with the Golden Fleece hanging from it. The priest did not move. The King went over to his chair and touched his hand. The old man half-opened his eyes.

'I thought you were dead,' said the King.

The priest replied: 'I might be at any moment, I might find myself in the next world. Just a slight noise or a sneeze might do it.'

The King drew a stool up and sat down. He looked affectionately at his confessor. 'I'll talk very quietly.'

'What's going on in the palace, to bring Your Majesty here at such an hour?'

'It's the same as always.'

'So?'

'I need to make my confession.'

Father Valdivielso's face showed as much surprise as it was possible for nearly motionless features to show.

'Confession on a Sunday afternoon? Has Your Majesty been up to one of his little games again?'

'As I said, Father, the same as always. I spent last night with a whore.'

'And you with such a pretty wife!'

'It's as though I didn't have one. They just let me see her every so often, and they let me sleep with her when it's a question of getting her pregnant because it so suits the State. But that's not something I decide: the people in charge take the decisions.'

'The Christian custom of having husband and wife sleep together avoids a lot of evils. Bodies get to know each other and can feel when one needs the other.'

'But certain people take a poor view of that.'

'And what if Your Majesty takes it into his head . . . ?'

'I do often take it into my head, but there are doors and procedures in the way.'

Father Valdivielso threw his arms up as far as he was able.

'God Almighty!'

'And then, you know . . .'

'Is there worse to come?'

'Yes, Father. I wanted to see the Queen naked.'

'And?'

'All laws both divine and human forbid it.'

'Human laws, I don't know much about them, but divine laws . . . Don't you realize that the first time a man and a woman got together they were naked?'

'But, Father, surely that was original sin?'

'That's what people who don't understand about that sin nor about others say. Eating from the Tree of Good and Evil never meant fornicating. That was what Adam and Eve had been doing pretty regularly ever since they met. I'm sure it was the very first thing they did. Logical, isn't it? That's what God had made them for.'

'Well, this morning, when I tried to get into the Queen's rooms, a cross was placed before me. So I, naturally . . .'

'Some people go to extremes!'

'But I find myself at their mercy.'

'It's not in my power to open or close doors, but if words of mine are any help to you, you may look at the Queen just as you wish, clothed or naked. She is the Queen, that's for sure, but she's also the wife of a young man.'

'I fear that even now my own conscience is clear, it may not be enough. Firstly, because I don't know what she thinks about it. What might they not have told her? Secondly, those doors . . .'

Father Valdivielso made a useless effort to sit up.

'Get down on your knees, Your Majesty, I'm going to give you absolution. The only thing I suggest is if you fail tonight, try again another night, and under no circumstances go back to whoring.'

The King bent his head, a dash of light fair colouring there among the shadows. Then he knelt down and the priest absolved him.

'Close the door gently, Your Majesty. As I told you, a loud noise might kill me. Though living on like this . . .'

When the King had gone down half a dozen stairs there appeared high up, almost touching the roof beams, a shaven, sly head. The head belonged to a man who climbed quickly down other staircases, rather unsafe, which creaked and swayed, though only gently. The spy with the hairless head went down without taking many precautions, and when the King was safely inside the labyrinth of passages and was beginning to get his bearings, a phlegmatic arquebusier with his gun on his shoulder went back up the same stairway, stopped at Father Valdivielso's door, and fired a shot – of gunpowder without a bullet – towards the beams in the roof. He replaced the smoking gun on his shoulder and went back down. The report raced round the empty spaces, passed through the lightly built walls, and surprised the King at a crossroads of passageways, wondering which way to turn. 'So the storm's got here! Won't it catch my confessor unawares?' The King selected the passage to the left, which left him precisely opposite the entrance to his own rooms. The soldiers on guard duty presented arms.

5

The usher went into the Minister's office by the secret door, or it may have been the backstairs door. He coughed, and when the Minister looked round, he bowed.

'The priest is here,' he announced.

'Does he wish to see me?'

'He said so, at least.'

'Then show him in.'

Father Villaescusa took his time about coming in, all tied up as he was in a series of bows and rosaries.

'What's the matter, Father?'

'A terrible misfortune, Excellency. When they took Father Valdivielso's supper up to him – he always eats in his room – they found him dead.'

'From natural causes?'

'It seems so, Excellency. He was wrapped up in a blanket in his armchair, as usual. A blanket, on a hot afternoon like this! It could be that he died of the heat.'

If the Minister perceived the irony in the priest's reply, he gave no sign.

'See to arrangements for the funeral, and let him be given a worthy burial.'

'We're attending to it, Your Excellency.'

'Was there something else, Father?'

'The late confessor will need a replacement . . .'

'That will take time, as you know. First and foremost, the King has to speak.'

'It's very likely that the King hasn't yet heard the news. He was seen going to his rooms just now.'

'As long as he stays there, we know where he is.'

'Have I then your permission to withdraw?'

The Minister looked rather distant, and for some moments did not reply. The priest respected his silence. Then the Minister said: 'Father Villaescusa, won't you sit down?'

'In my lowly station, Excellency . . .'

'Forget the courtesies. There, take that chair, put it in front of mine, and sit down.'

'If Your Excellency so commands . . .'

The Capuchin sat opposite the Minister, with the enormous desk between them. He kept his head lowered, but glanced at the Minister out of the corner of his eye. The latter seemed to have become lost again in his silence. While it lasted, the Capuchin clutched his rosary and began to mouth Ave Marias.

'That's enough praying for the moment, Father; you'll have time for that later. I need to consult you about something. In fact you already know the background. What I want to ask you is whether you have thought about my own case yet.'

'I was just then praying for a happy outcome for it.'

'And what have you come up with?'

'Since Providence seems not to listen to our beseeching, we shall have to use force on Her.'

'Force, on Providence?'

'Yes.'

'But isn't that sacrilege?'

'Can penances and sacrifices be sacrilegious?'

'No. I never heard them called that.'

'The solution I've come up with, the one I've just called forcing Providence's hand, is a sacrifice.'

'You'll have to be more explicit, Father.'

'I will be, if Your Excellency allows me to put certain questions.'

'That permission is implicit in the nature of this interview. I am consulting you as a theologian and a moralist.'

The Capuchin let go of the rosary he had been holding between his fingers, and crossed his hands on his chest. Then he in his turn fell professionally silent and made the Minister wait in tense expectation until he inquired: 'When Your Excellency goes to bed with his wife and copulates with her, does he feel any pleasure in the act?'

'The same as everybody else, nor more, no less.'

'And she?'

'To judge from the signs, Father, I think she does. Well, I'm sure she does, and most times, more than I do. In this matter women, Father, as you will know or will have heard, are a bit more demonstrative than we men. At least, they make more noise.'

The Capuchin put his hands to his head.

'My God, my God! It's allowable for men to feel carnal pleasure, but women should have no acquaintance with it, decent ones, I mean, whatever the moralists may say, they're never to be trusted. And I suppose she'll have undressed once or twice?'

'Probably more than once, Father. If she wants to, how can I refuse? When I got married, they told me about my duty to maintain conjugal harmony, and I was also told that women are the weaker sex and that one has to be understanding about them.'

The Capuchin gave him a hard look, as if all Jehovah's wrath were summed up in his expression.

'And in such circumstances you expect to obtain from the Lord the favour of having offspring? You hope to achieve the conception of those children of sin to whom the Psalmist alluded when he said *Et in peccato concepit me mater mea*?'

The Minister stared back at him, not angrily but uncomprehendingly.

'I was also told, Father, about the legitimate pleasures of matrimony.'

'I'm not blaming Your Excellency. I blame those who have the salvation of your soul in their charge. Is your confessor a Jesuit?'

'He was recommended to me by the Cardinal Primate of Spain.'

'Dodgy people, the Jesuits. They want to gain power over the world by being tolerant towards human weaknesses. In the Jesuits' eyes, all sins are venial, even in the very worst cases. In the report I'm drawing up for Your Excellency, about the session of the Holy Office we were discussing, I have a lot to say about the behaviour of a certain Jesuit, that Portuguese Father Almeida, a man who came from we know not where and whose destination is equally mysterious. He was the only one present to justify the King's carryings-on. Which, by the way, are not so very different from the ones Your Excellency has just been confessing to me.'

'The fact is, Father, that palace protocol has no influence in my private life, it doesn't affect me, and I don't think my personal sins can change the destiny of the subjects of this realm. The King and his sins are something else.'

The Capuchin thought hard, while his right hand felt for the crucifix on his rosary and clutched it.

'Indeed, the King and his sins are something else, and mis-behaviour by Your Excellency cannot affect the fate of the monarchy. But what about your personal destiny? Didn't they also tell Your Excellency that there exists one kind of morality for the people and a different one for its rulers? The nation needs some stimulus to get breeding, since without it we'd have no soldiers. But highly placed people are expected to conduct themselves differently. In top people the abuse, even the use, of fleshly pleasures, carries them into decadence. I could furnish Your Excellency with many instances, even within your own family.'

'But, Father, I haven't been looking for pleasures outside marriage. Not since I got married, at any rate.'

'I don't doubt that Your Excellency's way of life has been exemplary, but ask yourself whether the exemplary may not be that which is moral, nor even what is expedient. The exemplary is what is seen from outside. And what is it that is seen from outside? That Your Excellency doesn't keep a mistress and doesn't go whoring. That is all very well, but it isn't enough. One must be exemplary also in the face of the Lord, since it is the Lord who punishes or rewards. And the Lord is not giving Your Excellency children. Why not?'

'That's what I'm asking: why not?'

The Capuchin lifted the metal crucifix which his right hand was clutching up into the lamplight. 'There He is, crucified for us. What is Your Excellency doing to repay that sacrifice?'

n=段する

The Minister stared at the crucifix. Then he bent his head and moved it from side to side.

'Nothing in particular. I'm a man like everybody else.'

'We mortals can never know what God may be thinking, but we informed people can make a conjecture or two based on the circumstances. That's why, Your Excellency, I said we must force the Lord's hand.'

'And I didn't understand that.'

'Maybe I didn't understand myself. Now I think about it, I don't understand it, but I had some reason for saying it, and I wasn't just talking for the sake of it. We will force the Lord's hand, but on condition that you, and more especially your wife, give up the pleasure. On that condition, I will venture to do something which may produce the solution.'

'Something, what?'

'With Your Excellency's permission, I will leave that till tomorrow. Keep chaste till then.'

6

The Franciscan house had been built around a holm-oak tree, and the tree from that moment had offered a bench round its trunk to receive, though not too softly, the bottoms of those who wished to sit there and shelter from the sun. It was the younger friars in particular who used to seek that shade, but at the end of the day, at dusk, nobody ventured to sit there, nor even, almost, to cross the cloister, because it was rumoured that after sunset Father Rivadesella used that dark spot for his colloquies with the Evil One. Not that Father Rivadesella ever referred to him like that, calling him rather 'my mysterious interlocutor', though at times he allowed himself a few nomenclatural jokes, just in his mind, using names he had learned as a child in far-off Asturias, such as El Trasgu ('Old Nick'). That autumn evening the friar was late, on account of the session of the Holy Office, and when he crossed the sandy garden he was afraid Old Nick might have gone off, tired of so much waiting around. However that might be, he sat down in the darkest part, and had time to beg the Lord for the protection his soul – and possibly his body – would need if he was to stay at the devil's side without suffering major hurt. His prayer was brief but fervent, and then he still had time to feel desperate and to resolve to wait on for such time as might be deemed polite, and then to leave. His eyes scanned the darkness, piercing it, in his search for something in whose shape or body Old Nick might have installed himself, since he never appeared twice in the same way, though never doing so by using unpleasant or base objects either. He might be a cock that flew up on the bench and nuzzled his crest in the friar's habit, or a bird that flew into the refuge of his lap, or maybe a well set-up dog that licked his sandals. Once he'd been the biggest branch on the holm-oak, and another time a whirling wind that almost had a body. But never a creepy-crawly or a toad or a centipede. The dealings between the two, at least on Old Nick's part, had always been polite. Father Rivadesella on the other hand, assuming that the devil had no sense of smell, let off a good fart if he felt like it.

The friar was just about to leave when he sensed that, over to his left, the darkness was becoming more compact and taking on a roughly human shape. It resolved itself into a very tall, very thin man who sat down beside him and put one leg over the other.

Father Rivadesella crossed himself and said aloud 'Ave Maria Purissima', to which Old Nick replied: 'Don't be such an idiot. If it were a matter of faith, I'd tremble at that, but since it's only a superstition, it doesn't put me off.'

'A habit is a habit.'

'It's one you forget sometimes.'

This was true, but only up to a point. Getting accustomed to these colloquies, Father Rivadesella had lost his fear of hell and, with it, his sense of theatricality. He now talked with the devil as calmly as if he were talking to an old friend, and the words exchanged between them belonged rather to those customary in the secular world. In the same spirit the friar put his hands in his pockets and scratched his legs, which were itching with the heat.

'You'll be well aware of the fuss you've stirred up these last few hours.'

'I've some idea, but I didn't do the stirring. I'm just back from a long trip, I'm worn out, and I'm more convinced than ever (in case I wasn't before) that mankind is stupid up and down every latitude.'

'Well, your presence in the city has been made manifest in several ways, so to speak, so that even those with least brain-power could be aware of it. The parish priest of San Pedro's saw you last night floating way up in the sky, and you can't complain, since he said you were a handsome youth who sailed through the air and left a trail of silver behind you.'

'The parish priest of San Pedro's is a doddery old fool who sees visions. Last night I wasn't sailing through the sky, and there were no coupling witches nor anything of what that poor old fellow said he had seen. What happens is that with that spyglass he has, the clouds observed close up seem to him to be monsters. I can assure you that last night the sky over the city was free of daemons.'

'And what about that chasm in the Calle del Pez, through which mephitic sulphurous gases were coming up from hell?'

'Hell isn't in the centre of the earth, as people say, and as you say yourself when you preach, and it isn't full of combustible substances. Hell is cold.'

Father Rivadesella felt a sudden chill and was unable to speak. Eventually, he asked: 'Well, where is it?'

'Hell has no geographical location; it simply is, it exists. Just like heaven.'

'Then I don't understand.'

The moon had come out, dividing the space into two: one half of the cloister in darkness, the other lit, and there the light enabled Father Rivadesella to make out the outlines of the shadowy presence which, to his left, kept its legs crossed but moved its hands. Maybe it had a pointed beard, maybe not;

maybe it had long hair falling to the shoulders, as any gentleman might.

'If I were to maintain that thesis before a court, they'd send me to the stake.'

'It depends. If the proceedings were conducted in Latin, maybe they would. But if in Spanish, the differences between our two verbs for *to be* are very obvious.'

'Yes: but theological debates are conducted in Latin.'

'In that language too it is possible to distinguish between verbs for "being in some location" and "being meaning existing".'

'But not so clearly.'

The friar moved on his seat, as though ill at ease.

'Is this to be the theme for our meeting today?'

'The theme is up to you to propose.'

'Then what has got all us theologians worried is this whim of the King's, to see the Queen naked.'

'From my point of view, the subject has no importance. What difference can it make for him to see her naked or in a nightdress?'

'You really mean it's not a sin?'

'It's only a sin when it's done as a sin, and there's no sinful intention in the King's conscience. It's a question of simple curiosity and a legitimate wish.'

'Legitimate?'

'Why not? I can say at once that to me it's neither here nor there, and I imagine the Other would say the same. On these matters we're generally in agreement.'

'So: whether the King sees the Queen naked or not, it has nothing to do with the arrival of the fleet at Cadiz, nor with the defeat of our troops in Flanders?'

'The arrival of the ships at Cadiz depends only on whether the English get there in time to prevent it, and the defeat of Spanish arms in Flanders has mostly to do with the quality of their weapons, the discipline of the troops, and the positions of the contending forces. Given these factors, the general who knows how to use them best will win.'

'But doesn't prayer have some effect? There are intercessions going on in all the churches of the realm about the fate of the monarchy.'

'Sure. With no thought being given to the question of whether what you call the fate of the monarchy is a just or an unjust one. The Lord listens only to prayers which beg for mercy and justice, and you're neither just nor pious. You're merely Catholics.'

'But aren't you a Catholic too?'

'I am, but in my own way. I mean I'm a Catholic on the other side.'

Father Rivadesella scratched his head and said nothing, but against obstacles there was forcing its way into his mind a risky question, or rather than a question, a search for corroboration: 'So whether the King sees or fails to see the Queen's navel is a matter of no importance whatsoever.'

'Neither for God nor for me do kings and vassals exist, just men and women. There are no states or monarchies either. Those are just human inventions, and you try to involve us in your struggles. For us again there are neither Huguenots nor Catholics, neither Christians nor Turks, just people of good- or ill-will. It's the lot with the ill-will that concern me, and I'm fed up with them.'

Father Rivadesella had been crossing himself repeatedly. When the Evil One finished speaking, he was halfway through another crossing.

'Have you ever read St Augustine?' he asked.

'That's one who got away from me by a sheer miracle. Yes, I've read him, and found that he's right about some things but not about others.'

'Do you deny that Providence exists?'

'I understand it differently from you, and my way is the right one, according to my lights, and don't forget that although I lost the favour of the Other, I retain some good qualities. After Him, I am the most intelligent of beings.'

There fell a deep silence which seemed to make the whole garden darker still, perhaps because a cloud had stealthily obscured the moon. Father Rivadesella was inwardly delighted by circumstances which allowed him to conduct a dialogue, on an intimate basis, with the most intelligent being in all Creation after God Himself, all this without recourse to those bonds of obligation, ascetic self-denials, and sacrifices undertaken by those who spoke with God: colloquies from which they seemed not to derive much benefit, that is to say on the level of ideas, to judge by what they wrote later, since their whole effort had gone into ecstatic trances and swoonings, as if God were not intelligent but merely loving. Father Rivadesella's heart was not one of those that are easily moved, but his mind, henceforth, would be preoccupied by this new way of understanding History which did away with the Great Battle between God and the devil.

Then Old Nick said: 'Everything you're thinking now may lead you to erroneous conclusions. Let's leave it there and continue another day. Right now I've got to be off to Rome.'

'What have you got going on there?'

'I've let office business slide and my young assistant's affairs are going badly. I must go and give him a hand.'

'But isn't it enough for you to wish it and then everything is put in order?'

Old Nick stood up. The denser darkness of his body revealed a slim figure, one which, when he started to move, seemed quite willowy. It reminded Father Rivadesella of something, but, just as had happened that afternoon in the council chamber of the Holy Office, the only image that formed in his mind was that of a cockerel.

'I'm not allowed to perform any minor miracles. If I want to help someone I have to do it in ordinary ways, and that's not easy.'

7

Everything was in order, in the palace and in the monarchy as a whole. The courtiers were in order too, gathered in a big room where a Neapolitan quintet was playing. The Chief Minister cast a glance over the position of his papers on his desk, as he did every night on leaving, so that he would know the following day if anyone had been rummaging around in them, and in which. All entrances to the office had been locked on the inside, and the Minister left by a little door whose key reposed in his purse. In the anteroom the two ushers were dozing. He half woke them up when he called out, 'See you tomorrow!' A number of hats were doffed to him as he passed along the corridors, but the guards did not tap the floor with their halberds: he was still not a grandee, and in the King's presence, he still had to trail the plumes on his hat through the dust. Even so, people saluted him respectfully and looked at him fearfully. On the staircase down into the inner courtyard he coincided with his cousin the chief lady-in-waiting, who was also leaving. He asked her if she had a carriage: she answered that she had. He asked her if she had an escort: she answered that she hadn't.

'Come in my coach, then, and I'll take you home. At this time of night the city streets aren't all that safe.'

She accepted. The Minister helped her up the carriage step, and one of the footmen gave instructions for the Duchess's carriage to follow them. From the open window of his coach the Minister issued final orders: 'If you get couriers from Andalusia or Flanders, send them on to my house, whatever time it is.'

He closed the window and turned to his cousin.

'The fate of the monarchy turns on the news those two couriers may bring. Our fate does too, because if the fleet doesn't reach Cadiz, neither you nor I will collect our pay. The royal coffers are empty.'

'Then I'd like to know what the money is spent on, what with wages being so low, and the food being so bad, and even the Queen's dresses being the cheapest ones you can find in the market.'

'You don't realize how much goes on paying all the interest! Our creditors make off with more than half of what comes in!'

'And the wars?'

'Pah! Our soldiers live on what they steal.'

The carriage, escorted by four mounted arquebusiers, had

crossed the parade-ground and gone out through the gate. Groups of people didn't bother to look at them. Over here were some layabouts playing dice. Over there, a blind man with his guitar sang his versified satires, and if they weren't satires, miracle stories. Other groups of starving people were probably complaining, their indifference to the passing of the carriages showing their contempt.

The Minister observed: 'Nobody loves us.'

The Duchess replied: 'We don't give them much reason to love us.'

'That's how things are.'

'And they, the same as us, try not to get caught.'

Silence fell between them. The carriage bumped over the poorly cobbled streets. At intervals a lamp shed a flash of light on the two going home so late as they sat facing each other. The Minister crossed himself, but the Duchess didn't.

Eventually the Minister asked: 'And what's going on in the Queen's rooms?'

'She's stayed up, waiting for a warm bath.'

'A bath, you say?'

'That's right. The poor soul thinks her husband will visit her tonight.'

'You'll have left everything in good shape.'

'So far as I'm concerned, yes, though I hated doing it. It's not that I feel any lofty love for the Queen, but I'm sorry for the poor girl, all dressed up but lacking a sweetheart, as they say.'

'That's the way things have to be.'

'What I don't understand is by what right you meddle in such intimate matters. If the King and Queen want to sleep together, let them get on with it. If they want to strip off it's because they like it. If things turn out right, I'm intending to do the same tonight.'

'You're a clean-living widow. If you go in for fun-and-games, and it gets known, you'll be dismissed.'

'But I'm a young widow as well, and these hot nights one needs some company. That goes for cold nights in winter, too. In winter a body needs the warmth of a bedfellow.'

'And do you take a bath too?'

'Of course.'

'Aren't you afraid someone's going to report you?'

'The maid who helps me takes a bath too, and she isn't sleeping alone either. As for my servants, of both sexes, those that aren't Moors or judaizers belong to the Illuminati sect, and they shut up because they have to be careful anyway.'

'I call that surrounding oneself with security measures.'

'It's what one just has to do. You yourself say the city streets aren't safe. But is anything safe in the city? They say you're the most powerful man in the kingdom, but do you feel safe? Not even the King himself is!'

Outside there sounded a prolonged, authoritarian cry of 'Whoa!' and the carriage stopped. The four arquebusiers stationed themselves alongside, close to the windows.

The Minister put his head out: 'Is there some trouble?'

'It's a procession, Excellency.'

They had reached a crossroads. Down the street ahead of them were marching two lines of friars with torches, and between them, penitents with baulks of timber, chains on their feet, and whips that were flecking their shoulders with blood. They were praying in low tones, and every few Ave Marias there would come groans, cries of pain, exclamations: 'Have mercy on us, oh Lord! Direct that evil serpent away from us! Do not let your punishment fall upon your innocent people!'

At the end of the double line marched Father Villaescusa, in cap and surplice, bearing aloft a black cross whose base rested on his belt. They took their time to pass. Then the Minister's carriage went on its way towards the Duchess's house.

8

The King was able to catch a sideways glimpse of himself in the mirror, and despite the fear – or was it desire? – that made him tremble, he found himself able to approve, at least on a first impression, of the image which the mirror flashed back at him.

Then he studied himself full-faced and openly. He had donned a white suit, its only adornment being the highlights of the cloth itself, and by dint of using water and comb he had managed to discipline his mutinous fair hair which, well plastered down, topped off his figure nicely. From his neck there hung a miniature Golden Fleece: he was on the point of removing it but, since he intended to take a stroll around the great chamber where there would still be courtiers about, he decided to leave it and take it off later and keep it in his purse. He gave himself a smile and went out. On reaching the broadest of the corridors he could hear music coming from the big drawing-room, and went towards it. He did not fling the door open, nor did he allow himself to be announced. He pushed the door half-open, and could then see people dancing and beyond them, up on the dais, a troupe of musicians and singers. It seemed to him a good omen. He went in and glided along a wall without people noticing him, or, at least, without anyone giving a sign of having observed his entrance. He got himself into the embrasure of a window, almost hidden behind curtains, but someone was there already, whether from shyness or from a need to hide. This person took off his hat and swept it with a low bow. The King recognized him at once.

'This morning, Count, I ordered you to keep your hat on.'

'But this time, Your Majesty, you're not wearing a hat, and it would hardly be polite . . .'

'Thanks, Count. What's going on?'

'It's young Francisca Távora dancing alone in the middle of that group. She does it so well that everyone's watching her and beating out the rhythm by clapping hands.'

'She's good-looking too.'

'Yes, Your Majesty, she's lovely, and pretty scatter-brained, they say.'

'There's a lot of gossip in the court.'

'Sometimes with a basis in fact.'

'Aren't you tempted to dance? Or has that seafaring life not allowed you a chance to learn how to?'

'With Your Majesty's permission, I'd like to take the floor with the Portuguese girl.'

'Only on condition that I can watch you from here, without ceremony.'

'I promise Your Majesty it will all be very discreet.'

Count de la Peña Andrada bowed and left his hiding-place. Nobody observed his movements until he broke through the circle of courtiers and planted himself facing Francisca. He bowed to her and threw his hat in the air. The hat flew round the room and like a boomerang returned to the head from which it had set off. The courtiers uttered a unanimous gasp – 'Wow!' – and the Portuguese girl stopped her dancing.

'Will you allow me to dance with you?'

'If you can keep up with me . . . !'

The musicians had stopped playing, but they started up again at a sign from the Count. The circle spread out. Francisca took the initiative, but the Count followed her perfectly. Then the Count set the pace and the girl followed him, full of movement, infinitely supple, no way prudish about lifting her skirts and showing her lovely legs encased in purple stockings. The King from his hiding-place didn't miss a thing, admiring the skill and agility of the dancers and all the intricate posturings and points they indulged in, never before seen in the court. That is, until someone whispered to him: it was Colette, the Queen's chambermaid, suddenly there at his side. She didn't curtsy to him or go in for any other kind of ceremony. All she did was come close until her mouth was right against the King's ear, he having bent down.

'It's tonight, my lord, at eleven on the dot. Don't be late.'

She ran off, disappearing into the darkness near the door. The dancers went on with their mad game of come and go, give and take, offer and rejection, seduction and surrender, until Francisca could dance no more and sank to the floor, taking care to maintain the decencies, since she didn't reveal anything she ought not. The circle of courtiers applauded, the Count helped her to her feet, and as he did so, she slipped into his ear the message that she would expect him that night for a somewhat more private kind of dance: 'At eleven, eh? or thereabouts.'

Now on her feet again, Francisca curtsied to the public, and they clapped again. At that moment the King left his hiding-place and went over to the circle of courtiers. Everyone bowed to him, but the King went straight up to Francisca and said to her while she was curtsying: 'You dance wondrously well, my lady.'

She replied: 'And my partner didn't do so badly either.' Turning to the Count, she asked: 'Where did you learn how to dance?'

'In all those islands lost in the seas where men and women dance, but most of all, in the north of Portugal.'

A homesick tear or two clouded the girl's eyes.

'I might have guessed it. It's only there they dance with those points and interweavings.'

'A bit more to the north, too, my lady.'

'Are you from those parts?'

'Can't you tell from my accent?'

'The only thing I'd noticed was that when you talk it's almost as though you were singing.'

The King asked what time it was, and they told him a little after ten. 'On with the dancing!' he ordered, but Count de la Peña Andrada left the group of dancers and stayed at the King's side.

'Are you tired?'

Out of respect for the King's presence, they struck up a slow, ceremonious, and extremely boring pavane. Francisca did not take part, but made off into the depths of the palace. Count de la Peña Andrada pushed the King gently along, away from the crowd. With his hat in his hand still, he began to describe the dances of the naked women he had witnessed on the isles of the south seas, and what he had learned from them.

'And those women go about naked the whole time?'

'Yes, Your Majesty. The softness of the climate allows it.'

The Count got the notion that the King was sorry just then

not to be the ruler of one of those islands. To avoid increasing his depression, the Count changed the subject.

9

'And what did the King say to you?'

'He didn't actually say anything, but his face brightened as though a lamp had been lit inside him. Also, he straightened up, instead of looking droopy. It was as though the message had made another man of him.'

'Didn't he dance with the others?'

'No, he watched them from a corner, and didn't seem too cheerful about it.'

'Well: do you think he'll come?'

'I'm absolutely sure he will.'

The Queen's bed was big enough for four, but the fair and fragile girl needed only a corner of it. On it were spread out up to half a dozen nightdresses, all different in their cut, in their material, in their moral intention. The one that caught the attention was made of extra heavy stuff and covered in embroidery, and so rigid that it could have stood up without any support. It displayed at a certain place a hole with a sewn edging, and just above it, a scarlet cross, together with this legend in dark colours: 'Get thee behind me, Satan.' The Queen pointed to it.

'Should I put this one on? All the confessors so advise, and I know that some of my court ladies have similar ones.'

'With it being so stiff, my lady, you'd have trouble getting it off. And, you know, those words would repel the most ardent lover.'

'Well, which one do you recommend?'

The maid pointed to a garment of soft silk, nearly transparent, short and not too wide, which would come down to about mid-thigh on the Queen.

'This one, no doubt about it.'

The Queen covered her eyes with her hands.

'But that one hardly covers anything!'

'My lady, unless I've understood wrongly, the whole idea is to end up showing it all off.'

'That's right. But only at the end. I'm thinking of organizing a few little wrestling-matches for the King. One, naturally, at the very least, because he got out of the palace last night and slept with a tart.'

'Your mother, my lady the Queen of France, had clear proof that your father, my lord the King, was unfaithful to her with every woman he came across, and yet she never threw that in his face. Your mother, my lady the Queen, may have set a good example to follow in this case.'

'But I can't strip my nightie off just like that, because he asks me to. I have to wrestle a bit.'

'That being so, my lady, I agree, but on condition that every time Your Majesty says No she means Yes.'

'In Spanish or French?'

'I'd switch them around.'

The Queen picked up the nightdress Colette had selected: so flimsy was it that it fitted into her fist, and when she held it up and spread it out, she could see Colette through the material.

'If I wear this,' remarked the Queen, 'I'm afraid I shan't need to strip off.'

'That garment, Your Majesty, is a symbol, and symbols can be destroyed too.'

The Queen gathered up the other nightdresses and handed them to Colette.

'Take them away. How is my bath going?'

'Not warm enough, I fear.'

'The hot night suggests something cooling for the body. Are the doors properly locked?'

'Don't worry about that, Your Majesty. I know of lots of great dames here in the palace who take baths, and perfume themselves too. The men like them better that way.'

'The men might have an occasional wash too, and smell better.'

The maid opened a little door and went through it with her

lamp held high for the Queen. In the middle of the other room there was a bathtub of roughly human shape, full of water. The maid inspected the Queen closely, her lamp still held high.

'What are you staring at, Colette?'

'Nobody would guess Your Majesty has had a child.'

The Queen did not reply. She got into the water, carefully, first this, now that, then up to her waist, finally up to her neck. Colette put the lamp down on a chest.

'I'll go and look for the towel.' She went out noiselessly.

10

With a spyglass like this, brought as a present by some defeated admiral, you could clearly see, from the drawing-room window, the face of the clock on the tower of San Pedro, lit at that time by the moon. The King waited until there were only five minutes to go, put the spyglass down, and went out into the ante-chamber, where the guards had gone off to sleep. The King went by them on tiptoe, shut the door carefully, and once he was in his room he pushed up the latch which opened the door on to the corridor that would take him to the Queen's apartment. The latch worked, but the door, locked as it surely was, would not move. He tried nevertheless to force it open, twice, and gave up after a final effort, going back the way he had come but then turning into a very dark passageway which he followed to its end. At that point the door did open. It was the very door which, that morning, Father Villaescusa had sealed off with a cross. He found himself in a dark antechamber. When he closed the door behind him, he could hear prayers being said. On opening another door he found himself in a large room lit by four tall candles placed one at each corner of a coffin resting on the floor upon a black carpet. At the far end a group of friars with their cowls over their heads was praying quietly. The candles gave a good light on the coffin, and the King could recognize his confessor's face: the dead man was dressed in his friar's habit, with his hands joined over his breast and a small cross of smooth wood between them. The King hesitated for a moment, then knelt, stared at the corpse, covered his eyes with his hands, and said an Our Father somewhat disturbed by lustful images, half of them memories, half hopes. He was aware he was sinning, but then reflected that imagining his wife naked was no sin. He rose, crossed himself, and went across to the far door. There, however, the friars had grouped themselves compactly in front of it. He made several attempts to find a way through, finally exclaiming: 'Let me pass, I am the King!' But they made no move and no reply, and went on with their prayers. He made another effort, pushing this time, but they seemed to be made of stone, and were not only immovable, but weighty too. He stood there bewildered in the empty space between the coffin and the praying friars, wondering what to do. The little Latin he knew allowed him to recognize the penitential psalms among the prayers. They were not chanting, and the King felt an urge to join them and pray with them. But it seemed to him that the dead man's gaze was coming out through his eyelids and settling on him as it had done that afternoon, when the confessor had told him that it was no sin to see one's wife naked, and that instead of keeping their rooms and beds separate, they ought to sleep in the same bed, as ordinary folk do, so that their bodies could get to know each other and get used to each other: such was the order conveyed by God's law. The King genuflected to the coffin and went out through the door he had come in by, crossed the darkened anteroom, and found himself yet again in the same broad passageway. There were lots of doors, all locked. He had the feeling that the world was locked against him, that they had surrounded him with loneliness and silence, that the rooms and the person of the Queen were inaccessible. Then he began to cry.

'Tears won't take you anywhere, my lord,' said a small voice close to the King's ear. He recognized it as that of Count de la Peña Andrada.

'What are you doing here?'

'I'm on my way to a tryst, like yourself.'

'All the doors are locked.'

'Mine isn't, Your Majesty.'

'And how comes it you enjoy that privilege?'

'I am not the only one, my lord. Behind every locked door there is a bed and a couple of people in each. A few are legally married. Most are not. The bed that awaits me is not for a married relationship, naturally.'

'I guess it's that little fly-by-night Francisca de Távora.'

The Count replied with a slight bow.

'She's a very lovely lady, Your Majesty.'

'The Queen doesn't like her.'

'That's natural, my lord. A refined Frenchwoman and a boisterous Portuguese girl are not likely to get on well together. It's as if Your Majesty were to compare Camoens and Ronsard.'

'I've read a lot of Camoens, but I've never heard of the other one.'

'I'm sure Her Majesty the Queen knows his work off by heart.'

The King thought for some moments.

'Do you think the Queen will be expecting me?'

'Of course.'

'You know they've locked all the doors leading to her rooms?'

'Were it not so, Your Majesty, I shouldn't have found you in tears in this lonely spot.'

'So what shall we do?'

They were standing at the end of the passage next to a closed window. The Count pulled the shutters open and a diffused glow of moonlight came in.

'If we opened the glass part, we'd hear the heart of the sleeping city beating.'

'Well, open them.'

When the window was fully open, they could see part of the sleeping town in the moonlight. It was all very quiet.

'I cannot hear that heartbeat you mentioned, Count.'

'You have to lift the silence as you might lift a bedspread. Then you'll hear a distant hum made up of a thousand different sounds, from the scream of a man murdered in the darkness by some hired thugs to the moan of pleasure uttered by a girl who's just discovered love, her husband having gone off on a journey leaving her to resolve, at last, to receive the man who has been pursuing her as a lover. And, Your Majesty, that man has begged her to strip off. But there are also husbands who throw their wives out of bed because they've wanted to take their clothes off. Men and women in this city today are thinking of nothing else, since word got around that their lord the King wanted to see the Queen naked. This was talked about in every gossiping group, on every corner, in every convent parlour. It was not said, but it was alluded to, in the pulpits, and there are processions of penitents going round the city praying to God that His vengeance should not fall upon them for the King's sins.'

A slim white hand interrupted him.

'My confessor told me it wasn't a sin. Ah, by the way . . . my confessor died this very afternoon. Don't you find that suspicious?'

'Father Valdivielso's life was hanging by a thread, and a discharge of bulletless gunpowder snapped it. A lot of people thought it was a thunderclap. I thought the same, but then it occurred to me to sniff around a bit, and I'm one who knows what gunpowder smells like.'

'What do you think about all this?'

'The Inquisitor-General this afternoon set up no fewer than four committees to make recommendations about the matter. What is for Your Majesty simple and legitimate seems to them to be above all an affair of State. They see the devil everywhere – well, except for a few who don't believe he exists, but who find themselves forced to believe in him, because if they didn't, they'd be burned at the stake.'

The King said nothing. He was listening to himself now, but one could guess that this had something to do with bedspreads, since he said: 'Now I really can hear a gentle murmur . . .'

'Let's leave that now. If Your Majesty really wants to know what goes on in the city at night, ask for a report from your Chief Minister, who knows all about it. He knows there are people who murder for money, and he knows that in dives as deep as dungeons there are old whores that dance naked on the tables. He knows who is committing armed robberies, and who's cheating the coffers of the State. He is also informed about nuns' convents in which they love God and others in which they prefer those who come as lovers to their barred windows. Naturally he doesn't know about rapes, adulteries, virgins sold to lubricious old men with money, nor all the dirty doings and acts of vengeance and economies with the truth. But none of this matters at all. What worries the Minister is that your Majesty's sins may prevent the safe arrival of our fleet in Cadiz and the triumph of our arms in Flanders.'

'But what on earth can my sins have to do with that?'

'That is precisely what the four committees of theologians I mentioned have to determine.'

'And do you agree?'

'With the Minister? God forbid! With the Inquisition? As Your Majesty well knows, it's best to say nothing about that.'

It seemed a large rat was scrabbling about in a dark corner. The Count made a move to draw his sword, but the King stopped him.

'There's a lot of them around in the palace.'

'As big as that, not so many as Your Majesty thinks.'

He went over to the corner, kicked into the darkness, and a rat as big as a bearcub scuttled off.

'Now we can talk, my lord. I wish to offer Your Majesty my services.'

'For what purpose? Aren't you already serving me with a squadron of ships on some part of the coast?'

'I was referring to more immediate kinds of service. If Your Majesty permits, I will look into the question of arranging a meeting between Your Majesty and my lady the Queen, outside the palace and away from busybodies. In some place where locked doors protect and do not exclude.'

The King thought for a time.

'I'm beginning to think that's impossible.'

'I promise on my honour, on condition that the Queen is

forewarned and agrees with it. It's certain that at first light tomorrow her maid Colette will come and ask Your Majesty the reason for his absence tonight.'

'They'll have realized already that they're locked in.'

'Even so, Your Majesty ... It will be proper to warn the Queen from the start. How do I know the time I can set the meeting for? It's just one idea that I have . . .'

'Are you going to develop it in Francisca's arms?'

'Who knows, Your Majesty? Solutions come up in the most unexpected ways.'

'I wouldn't wish the Portuguese girl to know you found me in tears.'

'She won't, I assure you. But she, like everybody else in the court, is aware by now that the King was unable to reach the Queen's rooms. She knew that already, when we were dancing in the drawing-room.'

'They were all in it, then?'

'In a way, yes.'

A door in the corridor opened, and the white figure of a woman appeared, with a lamp held aloft. She looked up and down.

'Lady Francisca is getting restless, Your Majesty. I'm going off duty now.'

'I wish you luck.'

The Count bowed once more.

'Expect me tomorrow, Your Majesty. Don't leave the palace for any reason whatsoever.'

He drifted away into the darkness, towards the door from which the woman in white had emerged. The King heard something like 'Wait a bit, I'm here.' The door closed. The King went over to the window, to listen to the night. The shadow of the rat as big as a bearcub scuttled noiselessly along the passage, sticking close to the wall.

11

The table at which the Chief Minister and Lady Barbara were dining was made of rare woods brought from the Indies and worked by good carpenters. It stretched out down the large dining-room, needing four candelabra to light it properly. There were eight when guests were present. A huge linen tablecloth brought secretly from Ireland by Catholics seeking asylum covered it and hung down at the sides. There were twenty chairs, but only two, one at each end, were occupied: their backs were decorated with the arms of the Minister as a second son, and those of his wife as a titled lady. Further signs of nobility were scattered round the room on hangings and tapestries. The four servants on duty, two behind his chair and two behind hers, wore the livery of the master of the house, already well-known in the court though only from a short time past. The distance and the intervening lights made conversation difficult, but it was easy to exchange glances, hers passionate, his full of obligatory chilliness.

When they folded their napkins she stood up, went over to him, kissed him on the cheek, and said: 'Don't be long!'

He answered: 'Don't expect me. I've a lot of work on hand. It would be best for you go and pray.'

She withdrew sadly, disposed to pray until she fell asleep, to pray a good part of the night.

The Minister rose as soon as she had departed, and went out through the door opposite, preceded by two lackeys with their lamps. He opened the door into his office and ordered them to follow. When they had provided light for the room, he sent them off with this order: 'I'm awaiting some news. Whoever it is who comes, wake me up even if I've gone to bed.'

There were two maps spread out on his enormous desk. One was of the coast of Cadiz, extending from near Lisbon to the Straits of Gibraltar. The other was of Flanders. On both were traced circles and black and red marks, showing where the squadrons of the fleet were, and where the armies. On the sea

chart the Minister used a pair of compasses to calculate the
nautical miles which still lay between Cadiz and the fleet which
had sailed from the Canaries, and the distance between that fleet
and the English one sighted days earlier off Cascaes. The
measurements were the same. In all logic, the two had to clash.
Faced with the map of Flanders, however, the Minister felt his
lack of expertise, since he knew nothing of tactics and strategies
on land, and the compasses in his hand were no use. Red dots,
black dots, more red dots than black. He'd already forgotten, or
at least was in doubt about it in his confusion, which indicated
which side. He ought to have brought some of those pensioned-
off old soldiers along, some lame, some armless, who had kicked
their heels for months past in his waiting-room hoping he would
reward their services. Some had been major-generals, most of
them mere captains. At the time he'd never thought they could
be of any further use to him.

He tried to capture impressions of the fleet as it lay shattered,
of bullion sinking into the depths, of fortresses stormed, of
starving, fleeing troops. He strove to fix them in his mind, with
the aid of the maps spread out on his desk, but they were
quickly pushed aside by thoughts of his wife waiting for him in
bed, perhaps moaning, perhaps naked in order to stimulate him
the more. He crossed himself, trying to banish the images, but
they persisted, they moved, they made sounds. He sought a
remedy in a devotional book, but he couldn't see the words,
only the images which superimposed themselves, insistently
seductive. It occurred to him to flagellate himself as a remedy,
and he rose to look for a bit of rope with which to lash his back,
even though he'd stay dressed. At that moment there came a
knock at the door. The images disappeared at once. He called
'Come in!', and a servant entered.

'There's a friar come, sir. And since Your Lordship said he'd
receive any visitor at any time . . .'

'A friar at such an hour?'

'Yes, Excellency. Father Villaescusa, a Capuchin.'

'Show him in at once.'

He felt suddenly calm, certain that, with Father Villaescusa present, his mind would be free of impure desires. He heard the friar's sandals softly crossing the floor of the anteroom, and then he appeared in the doorway, head humbly down, hands crossed in his sleeves, his head bare.

'Your Excellency!'

The Minister told him to sit down, which the friar did with a show of unwillingness. He asked him if he wanted something to drink, and the friar said 'No'.

'May one ask to what this late visit is owed?'

The friar had kept his head lowered, as if it were sunk on his chest. He raised it now, like a cock showing off its crest.

'Your Excellency, our whole plan is in disarray.'

'Could it be, perhaps, that the King found a door open?'

'No, Excellency. The King is wandering about the palace corridors, hoping the devil will work some miracle for him. But the miracle will come from another direction. That damned Count de la Peña Andrada has promised to fix a meeting with the Queen for him outside the palace. Tomorrow, tomorrow as ever was.'

'Why did you call him damned?'

'Because there can be no doubt he's the devil's instrument.'

'A believer defends himself from the devil with prayers.'

'Yes, Excellency, but our proverb says it plainly: "Praying is fine, but keep bashing away with the hammer."'

'I don't doubt, Father, that the old saw is right, especially when you quote it. However: which is the hammer, and what are we going to hit with it?'

'Count de la Peña Andrada is at this moment having a good time with a lady in the palace. It'd be easy to pick him up with an order for his arrest. That's why I've come.'

'You know that the King, a few hours back, ordered the Count to put his hat on?'

'Everyone knows, Your Excellency. It's a reward for all his pimping. Besides, the King doesn't have to know about any arrest. I know plenty of places in the palace where the Count could be held in secret. I would undertake the duty of having him conveyed there.'

'And after that . . . ?'

'When the Holy Office has come to a decision, it would take charge of him. In secret, again. There are people in the dungeons in the Plaza de Santo Domingo whose families have long since given them up for dead, and who have Masses said for their souls.'

'I didn't know that.'

The Minister went over to a side-table, jotted something on a piece of paper, waited for the ink to dry, and handed it, unfolded, to the friar.

'Is this all right, do you think?'

The friar read it aloud: 'For the better service of the monarchy, and by order of His Majesty, our lord the King, I order that His Excellency Count de la Peña Andrada be arrested and imprisoned, in the greatest secrecy, until further notice.' The friar raised questioning eyes: 'By order of His Majesty the King . . . ?'

'It's the standard formula.'

The friar folded the paper and tucked it away.

'Now, Excellency, there were two other matters . . . One can certainly be left till tomorrow. The other can't be delayed. It would in any case have forced me to come here at this unseemly hour, even at the risk of disturbing Your Excellency.'

'Which is the matter that can wait?'

'That report, my lord. The detailed account of what took place this afternoon in the Supreme Council of the Inquisition.'

He took out a roll of papers and held it out to the Minister, who placed it on his desk without looking at it.

'That can wait, then, till tomorrow. And the other one?'

'Your Excellency, accompanied by his wife, should present himself tomorrow at ten in the morning in the church of the San Plácido convent. I shall be there to hear your confession. What may happen thereafter, or rather, what you'll have to do, will be told you in due course.'

'Why San Plácido?'

'Because Your Excellency is patron of the convent, and because the Mother Superior, for certain reasons I know about, will be there to help us.'

The Minister thought of the deep shame his wife would feel on having to confess her conjugal failings to this implacable friar.

'Is there no way but this, Father?'

'I told you this morning that we must force God's hand. I am certain that God himself suggested this solution to me.'

'If you say so, Father . . .'

The friar rose.

'At ten, then, on the dot, in the church in the Calle de San Roque. You're not to come by some secret passageway either – I know they exist – but in broad daylight, in your carriage. Don't conceal yourself in any way, and don't offer any explanations, not even to your wife.'

The friar made as if to leave, but the Minister stopped him.

'One moment, Father. The city streets are unsafe. My carriage can take you to the palace, with an escort.'

The friar bowed and offered his thanks.

The square in front of the palace was in darkness. The carriage with its four arquebusiers were shadows entering that realm of shadows. At the main gate a postern door was opened for them. The Capuchin put his head out of the window.

'I have a message from His Excellency the Chief Minister for the commander of the guard.'

A man came to help him down the carriage step, and the coachman asked if he was to wait.

'No, I'll spend the night in the palace.'

A lamp was lit in the postern, and under it there appeared the commander of the guard, still doing his breeches up. Father Villaescusa handed him his paper, without greeting him. The officer asked for a light so he could see to read, and a torch was brought. Meanwhile the carriage and its escort lumbered off.

'Where should we look for this gentleman?'

'He'll be in the palace, and I'll take you to him. Bring half a dozen soldiers and come with me.'

'As many as that, Father?'

'You don't know what sort of devil we've got to handle. You could bring eight, we'd be safer. Eight men with arquebuses.'

'I don't have guns, Father. Just halberds.'

'Well, halberds, then, but held by strong arms.'

'All those assigned to the palace are pretty tough.'

The officer shouted an order for a squad of eight halberdiers to assemble. In two files of four men each, with the officer and the friar between them, they began to climb the main staircase.

12

From outside they hammered on the massive door with the butts of their weapons, and a voice with an exaggeratedly harsh tone shouted: 'Open up, in the King's name!'

Count de la Peña Andrada sat up in bed with a jerk.

'They've come for me.'

'How do you know?' asked Francisca, also now sitting up bare-breasted.

'Because the King's officers can't have anything against you.'

'But you're his friend.'

'Sure, but after the King, nobody's going to do me any favours. Even if the King were to make a show of justice, those who are to carry it out would act as if they were unaware of his wishes.'

'So you'll let yourself be arrested?'

'There may be some means of escape. Right now, get up, and I'll do the same.'

They hopped out of bed on different sides. The Count began to get dressed with all speed, while she asked what she should do.

'Put that white dressing-gown on and find the biggest candelabrum you can in these rooms. When I open the door, you stand close by with the light held high.'

Outside, the bangs on the door and the shouts continued.

'Tell them to wait.'

'I'm getting dressed, gentlemen. Please be patient.'

Now the Count was fully dressed.

'When I've drawn the bolts back, tell them to come in.'

He pulled at the bolts. They were well greased, and made no sound.

'Come in.'

As the door was opened, it concealed the Count behind it. The friar and the officer could be seen in the half-dark passage. The soldiers with their halberds stood further back. The officer said: 'I have an order for the arrest of Count de la Peña Andrada.'

'But why are you looking for him here? I don't know anybody of that name, and I don't receive visitors at times like this.'

The friar stepped boldly forward.

'We're sure he's hiding in there.'

'Then come and take a look.' As the friar stretched his arm out to push her aside, Francisca added: 'But without touching a single thread of my clothes! Anybody that does, I'll poke his eyes out!' Her blazing eyes stopped the friar in his tracks.

'Please let me pass.'

'The door is open for you.'

The soldiers went in too. Francisca, a silent statue full of fury, turned her back on the door as if to light the way for them. Two soldiers stayed back on guard, while the others, together with the friar and the officer, poked about everywhere looking for the Count or for signs of him. They found nothing.

'Your Ladyship will have to come with us, to give evidence,' the friar ventured.

'So you have an order against me too?'

'No, but one thing follows from the other.'

'I'm a lady-in-waiting to the Queen and a member of the House of Távora. Nobody can arrest me, though you could expel me from the country if His Majesty so orders. However, getting me expelled would take a lot of paperwork, so I bid you good-bye and hope you'll leave me to sleep in peace. Tomorrow I'll make my protest, and we'll see what comes of that.'

She spoke with such force and authority that the officer looked at the friar and they both backed away towards the door, followed by the soldiers. They went out and closed the door. Francisca put her lamp down on a corner of the table and began to look for the Count, calling to him in a low voice.

'Where are you? They've gone now, you can come out.'

Now she was by the door they had just closed, and next to the stretch of wall against which the Count had flattened himself when the friar and his men had opened it up. She thought she could see on the wall the outline of a tall man with a sword and a hat with a long plume, just like the Count: the silhouette – a bit fuzzy, naturally – which someone would have left on filtering through the wall. She moved the lamp closer and the shape disappeared, but when she moved the lamp away, she saw it again: a very dashing outline, its edges sharper now that she observed it squarely, but fading again when she viewed it obliquely. The Count seemed to smile at her from the dark depths of time. 'It's the devil!' she shrieked. 'I've been sleeping with the devil!' Lady Francisca de Távora ran through her rooms with her hair flying wildly, shrieking 'It's the devil! It's the devil!' Finally she fell exhausted on the bed, praying away and groaning. She didn't notice how, on hurling herself down on the ruffled sheet, she'd left her thighs exposed.

13

'It's not good manners to be so late,' said the Queen.

Colette agreed: 'No, it's not very polite.'

'How about you going off to look for the King, Colette? Tell him his wife is waiting for him. Not best pleased, but still waiting.'

'I think that's altogether too considerate, but I'll go.'

Colette left the bedroom and went to the door through which the King should have entered. It was locked. She checked all the others through which it was generally possible to get out of those inviolable rooms, but they were all locked too. She shook them all hard, one after the other, but they were strong and secure. On the other side of one of the doors she seemed to hear a psalm being sung. 'My God!' she cried in her native French, and then ran back to the bedroom.

'We're prisoners, my lady! The doors won't open either way! I can't get out, and the King can't get in!'

'But why, dear Lord, why?'

'Your Majesty: in this court it's the devil who rules, even though some think it's God. There's someone very high up who's concerned to prevent the King coming to visit you tonight.'

'But why, dear Lord, why?'

The Queen, sitting on the huge bed in the flimsy nightdress she had chosen for the encounter, was in tears.

'The awful thing, Your Majesty,' said Colette, 'is that I too had an appointment at eleven, and I can't get to it either.'

14

Count de la Peña Andrada leapt out of his carriage and rapped with his knuckles on the postern beside his main door. A servant with a lamp opened it at once.

'Has anybody been asking for me? Have any soldiers been around?'

'No, Excellency. There's just a woman who's waiting in the courtyard.'

Lucretia had fallen asleep in the armchair they offered her to ease her wait. The Count touched her and she awoke with a start.

'What are you doing here?'

'My lord, the Inquisition thugs have shut and sealed up my mistress's house. I spent the evening looking for somewhere to sleep, but I couldn't find a safe place. That's why I've thrown myself on your hospitality.'

The Count lifted her in his arms.

'You'll sleep in a good bed, alone or with company, as you prefer.'

And he called to the servant: 'Will you light the way for us?'

The servant set off up the broad stairs with their bright marble and baroque decoration. He went into the Count's rooms and set the lamp down. The Count put Lucretia down on the floor and indicated the bed.

'There you are. You can wait with your eyes open or closed.'

'Open, my lord, wide open, if it's all the same to you.'

'As you wish. I'm off to look for a certain Jesuit I have to speak to. I'll be back as soon as I can.'

Lucretia began to undress, draping her clothes over a chair. Then she crossed herself hastily and got into bed. In the distance, though still inside the house, she heard a window slam. Then the wind began to moan. It came down from the mountains like a herd of horses suddenly let loose, sweeping down howling round the corners and chilling the warm night air. Lucretia, half asleep, wrapped herself up in the bedclothes as best she could.

CHAPTER FOUR

I

Marfisa had listened half-asleep, though agreeably enough, to the chants for tierce. She knelt, stood up, and sat down mechanically, obedient to the taps which the Mother Superior gave with her stick on the woodwork of her high chair in order to indicate the posture demanded by each prayer. Rather, she watched the other nuns and did what they did. When the service was over she fell into step with one of the lines of nuns which perambulated the cloister for a while. Then she found herself alone, and went to her cell. When she opened the door she beheld a gentleman dressed in black who at once stood up. Marfisa did not cross the threshold.

'What are you doing here?'

'Come in, don't be alarmed. I am Father Almeida, of the Society of Jesus, and we must have a talk.'

'How did you get as far as this, and with whose permission?'

'I entered urged on by necessity and following the secret passages. Haven't you heard talk of them? In the court everybody knows about them, and I think they do in the city as well.'

'The famous passages! So it is true?'

'Well, you see me here before you.'

Marfisa turned the key in the lock and advanced into the middle of the room.

'Well now, do sit down, if you're a Jesuit as you say you are. Please talk very quietly – these walls may be thick, but everyone knows about what is said the other side of them.'

'It's essential that no one should hear about what I've come to tell you.'

'Not even myself?'

'You'll do well to forget everything about it as soon as it's happened.'

'Everything, but what?'

'You'll very soon know.'

Marfisa sat on the edge of the little bed.

'Then get on with it.'

Marfisa had drawn her headdress well down over her face, but not so much as not to leave a chink through which she could study Father Almeida – very handsome, very well set-up – at her leisure. She did not dare to imagine he would have come to the convent in order to make her some professional proposition, though she wished he had done. In any case the priest, on close inspection, had the face of an angel rather than of a layabout. 'But he won't know who I am,' she told herself as she resolved to dismiss her desires and think of something else. The Jesuit remained courteous and remote. He didn't look at her. When he did address her, he did so as though he were seeking a listener up in the air.

'You know the King, I believe?'

'How do you know that?'

'That doesn't matter now. I've come to tell you that there's a plot in the palace to prevent the King sleeping with the Queen, and that some people, myself among them, are trying to defeat the plot.'

'Who sent you here?'

'Your friend Count de la Peña Andrada.'

'That rogue!' exclaimed Marfisa, moving her veil so her face could be seen. 'He came pimping so the King could sleep with me, and now he wants to get the man back into the marital bed. Well, he might have thought of that earlier, and in particular, he might have avoided dropping me in the soup. It all comes out in the end, and it's poor little me that has to pay for the damage.'

'So far as you're concerned, there's nothing to be done. The Holy Office is on your tracks, and they'll soon find where you're hiding. But since the Count and I will be hunted down too, we've thought it a good idea to take you with us, that is only so far, to a place from which you'd go one way and we another. We'd leave you in good hands.'

'Just fancy that! The gentlemen plan to abandon me in the middle of the desert, so I can purge my sins there. Well, include me out!'

'We can talk about that later. The question right now is whether the King and Queen will be able to meet in privacy.'

'My house, as you know, has been shut and sealed by the Inquisition thugs.'

'We thought the meeting might take place here.'

'Here? Right here in the convent?'

'Here, young lady, means in this very cell.'

Marfisa glanced about her.

'Yes, it's just the sort of place for the King and Queen to get together!'

'For them it'll be quite as lovely as paradise itself.'

Marfisa seemed to ponder, or maybe she was simply remembering.

'Look at it this way, Father. Even in the middle of the finest garden, the King won't know what to do with the Queen.'

'Well, she's not all that experienced either.'

'But any woman, even the youngest virgin, expects something the King is not capable of giving.'

'Neither you, nor I, nor the Count is to blame for that.'

Marfisa bent her head and said softly: 'Given a few more nights, I could have set him to rights.'

'But that setting to rights, young lady, is not proper morally, and palace protocols are against it too. You can't imagine how awful the guardians of the rules can get! A good part of the blame for what's happened is theirs.'

'And the other part is mine.'

'How do you know?'

'It's not that I know, but I can smell it. From certain things that happened . . .'

'It's on account of those things that the King is set upon seeing the Queen naked.'

'And it's got to be here?'

'We talked it over a lot, and that's the conclusion the Count and I came to.'

'A pretty pair you make!'

With an unexpected movement, Marfisa tore off her head-dress. She shook her head, and the shower of her golden hair fell to her shoulders.

'Since you know who I am . . .'

The Jesuit seemed to be concentrating on a late-flying insect which was buzzing about in a corner of the ceiling.

'Right, you tell me what you want me to do.'

'We thought you should take charge of picking up the Queen from the palace and bringing her to the convent. For that, it's essential for the Mother Superior to give her consent, but we don't doubt her goodwill or her devotion to the monarchy. Remember, she's of the blood-royal. It's also the case that, according to what we hear, she'll be very busy around midday with another matter, somewhat less respectable, one she can't get out of. Maybe even downright scandalous. Since it's all out in the open, as you very properly remarked yourself, the court gossips will have to choose what they want to feel outraged about, and what they want to find amusing, twice over, that is.'

'About picking up the Queen: how will I manage that?'

'I'll be waiting for you in a blacked-out carriage, just behind the convent, you know, in the square. If the King and Queen are to get together at twelve, it will be fine if you appear in the square at half-past eleven.'

'But how am I going to get out of the convent? It's an enclosed Order, as you must be aware.'

'That's simple. You just open the door and go.'

'Oh, sure. That hadn't occurred to me. All very simple. I open the door and go.'

'And if you happen to run into a lot of people as you go out, don't worry, no one's going to to be surprised at seeing a nun outside the convent.'

'Right! It's perfectly normal to see a nun out in the street looking for a carriage!'

'You may not think so, but you'll see it really is so.'

Father Almeida rose, bowed lightly to Marfisa, and went to the door. She followed him and watched as he made off through the cloister, completely calm, so sure of himself. When the Jesuit had disappeared down one of the secret passages Marfisa went to the Mother Superior's room, but a nun told her that she was engaged in a confidential discussion with a Capuchin Father loaded with lots of religious bits and pieces. Marfisa hovered around, killing time.

2

Father Villaescusa had unfolded to the Mother Superior – who listened in attentive amazement – all the arguments about reasons of State and personal need in support of the proposition that the hand of Providence should be forced so that the Chief Minister's wife should produce a son or, failing that, a daughter. He furthermore insinuated that it had undoubtedly been the Lord, in His divine wisdom, who had inspired in him the plan whereby the Minister's wife could be made incontrovertibly pregnant, from which act there would come great benefits for the commonweal and for the younger branch of the Guzmán family – that is, not the Andalusian branch, the Madrid one. Without that blessing from on high the family would become extinct, and the favours the Minister expected to receive from the Crown would pass to collaterals with whom he was not on good terms. The only argument that persuaded the Mother Superior was, however, that which concerned the Minister's patronage of her convent, it being natural that her chapel should be the one selected for this perilous experiment which Father Villaescusa called forcing the hand of Providence, but which she, in her plain language, called shameless sacrilege. Eventually they agreed a method and a time. Father Villaescusa left the convent and set off in the carriage which had brought him there at such an early hour for the Chief Minister's residence, where the anxious couple awaited his final decision.

Marfisa watched him go, so smug, and only when the friar

was well out of sight did she venture to knock at the abbess's
door. Mother de la Cerda called to her to come in.

'What brings you here so early?'

Marfisa felt awkward and took her time to get around to
explaining the plan Father Almeida had put to her.

'Well, I don't know what there is about my convent, but
everybody has chosen it as the most suitable place in which to
unravel their entanglements.'

'I must tell the Reverend Mother that in the palace there's a
real conspiracy to prevent the King and Queen being alone
together.'

'But what am I going to get out of all this fuss?'

'I suggest you should ask the King for a new clock for the
convent. I've noticed that the present one is all over the place.'

'That's not a bad idea, Marfisa. However, as I see things, I'm
not going to get a chance to speak to the King. There's another
very delicate matter that'll keep me occupied at precisely the
same time.'

'If Reverend Mother gives me permission, I'll make the request
to the King myself.'

The Mother Superior, born a de la Cerda, that is of unques-
tionable blood-royal, thought for a while.

'It's the least my cousin the King can do for this convent.
Don't forget to remind him who I am, since he's likely to have
forgotten.'

'Or he never did know, Reverend Mother.'

'And when all this is over, what are you going to do?'

'The first thing is, I shall leave the convent, so that if they
question you, you'll be in the clear. After that, who knows?
Women in my profession never have their future plainly marked
out.'

'You deserve the best, Marfisa. If at some stage you tire of
your life and need a calm refuge, don't forget this place. You
could live and die in this convent and nobody would have any
suspicions about your past.'

'My past? It's my future I'd like to know about.'

'Right. So we're agreed that, while all the nuns are in the

choir, about midday, you'll get the Queen into your cell. The
King will follow, and after that it's all up to them. That's what I
wanted to say to you.'

3

Father Villaescusa went off in thrall to the spirit of speed, a
beneficent one, doubtless. His carriage shot along the city streets
as if the wheels and the horses' hooves weren't touching but
rather flying over the uneven cobbles, full of potholes and
stinking puddles. He reached the palace and – without descend-
ing from the carriage – left a message for the Chief Minister to
say that everything was ready, and that the appointment in the
San Plácido convent was for ten o'clock. Then he went back to
the convent and began to issue orders. Neither bishops nor
priests on visitations had issued them so authoritatively.

Father Almeida's carriage was not far behind the other, but
instead of stopping at the main gate of the palace, it went on to
a little side door where they let him in after hearing the password
from him. He managed to find his way about in the seemingly
endless series of corridors that all looked the same whichever
way one looked, and eventually he reached a door which Colette
opened to him.

'What are you doing here, Your Reverence?' she asked in a
mixture of French and Spanish.

The Jesuit answered in excellent French: 'Tell your mistress to
be ready at about half-past eleven tomorrow, dressed in something modest and prepared for a trip in a coach to take her to a
meeting with the King, in a discreet spot far from the conspira-
cies of the court. I will come myself, accompanied by a nun, to
pick her up. You have to persuade her to do it, and to trust us.
Under her modest outer dress, she's to wear her best lingerie,
the set she brought from Paris that they won't let her wear here.
And tell her not to lose hope.'

'And you, Father – what do you have to do with all this?'

'I am here to see that the King and the Queen can meet and

make love as husband and wife, not as King and Queen. All the rest is up to Providence.'

'I don't trust people who talk about Providence.'

'Well, in that case, you don't have to worry. At last the King and Queen will find a place where they can meet in private.'

'And the King – does he know about all this?'

'He knows, and he agrees.'

'Then Your Reverence ought to know I don't trust that young man. He's a softie. If he had real character, none of these machinations would be necessary. In what part of the world has it ever been the case that, for a husband to be with his wife in private, the protocols and even the clergy have to come into it?'

'In this part of the world where we are, such things and even greater miracles are ten-a-penny. Don't lose your sense of reality.'

'That's right, Father. But I wish all this were happening in Paris!'

'Ah, Paris . . . !'

4

The Chief Minister left his office through the secret door, after giving orders that nobody was to disturb him. He went out of the palace by a little-used exit, on the side opposite to that which Father Almeida had used. He went to his house in an ordinary carriage that was waiting for him, and there at his door his personal coach stood waiting, decorated with his arms and escorted as was normal: mounted arquebusiers, servants on foot, liveried lackeys decked out in buttons and bows. A lot of common people had assembled to see the spectacle. They watched the Minister get out of his carriage and go into his mansion, to emerge shortly with his wife on his arm: she was dressed entirely in black, without jewels or plumes to enhance her beauty, a little downcast but also a mite hopeful. The Minister's lady was middling tall, and her dress, however severe, did not hide her charms. To the men of the common sort this

well-covered woman with her undulating walk was highly
attractive. They pictured her in bed, though would not have
cared to confess such thoughts. 'Some bird!'

The morning was chilly now. As he got into the carriage the
Minister sneezed.

'Are you cold?' he asked his wife.

She answered: 'Don't worry. I'm well wrapped up.'

The carriage started off, with its mounted escort and followed
by the servants on foot. They travelled in silence, and didn't
look at each other either. After a long spell of rattling along the
bumpy streets, she took his hand and asked: 'Shall we manage
it?'

To which he replied: 'It'll be a bad day if we can't. And God
will help us.'

She sighed and fell silent again. In silence they arrived at the
convent. The servants on foot had driven the idle onlookers
away. They got out and went into the church holding hands.
The church was empty, very white except for the black saints on
their statue-bases. The only person there was a shadowy but not
black figure waiting for them next to the altar: a chubby friar,
bald, aquiline, almost the exact profile of Caesar himself. The
Minister thought, as he went forward up the central aisle hand
in hand with his wife, that this friar was made to rule, and that
what he was after was in fact a chance to rule. The Minister was
not too pleased. None the less, he went forward, and knelt on
the altar steps. His wife at once did the same. The friar had not
moved. They bent their heads and began to pray, the Minister
leading and she saying the responses. The friar listened to them
for a moment and then disappeared. The church was really
empty now. *Adjutorium nostrum in nomine Domini. Qui fecit
caelum et terram . . .*

5

Marfisa thought her cell was too cold and too dark. She got
permission from the Mother Superior to do something about it,

and spent a lot of time wangling candlesticks, a good stove, and
a pair of extra blankets. She went down to the garden and, by
scraping about in thickets and plots, was able to put together a
bunch of ordinary flowers, which she put in a jar of water on a
corner of her table. Then she swept the floor and left it without
a single speck of dust. She left lighting the candles till later. Then
she looked round her cell and considered that as a nuptial
chamber it still left a lot to be desired. She still hadn't found
anything to hand with which to decorate it and banish some of
its severity and bareness. The church hangings were in the
charge of the chaplain, and Marfisa wanted to have nothing to
do with him, and didn't care to inform him about the changes
she had made in the decorations of her cell, and still less about
their purpose. It struck eleven. She threw off her nun's habit,
dressed in man's clothes, and put her habit on again over that.
She couldn't think where to hide her hat, and had to carry it
with her, resolving to leave it on some seat in the church. She
sat for half an hour but did not wait for the chime of the convent
clock, which was always slow. As she entered the church she
could see in the presbytery the figure of a man kneeling. It
wasn't the King, naturally. She put the hat down and went over
to the door. Out in the street were lots of people and horses,
and a luxurious coach. People were chatting, or just waiting by
the wall, and a couple of layabouts were playing dice on the
ground. Nobody noticed her, or, at least, nobody paid her any
attention. When she got round the corner she could see the
Jesuit's carriage. She got in, and the vehicle moved slowly off.

6

The Minister went over to Father Villaescusa with a step he
hoped was firm. The priest's face seemed to have gathered to
itself all the gravity of which he was capable, till it had assumed
the texture of stone, immobile and grim.

'Kneel down.'

The Minister knelt on a hassock covered in red chenille.

'Before the Holy Tribunal of Penance, there are no hierarchies and no titles. There is simply a humble penitent and this representative of the power of the Church, which binds and unbinds everything. That which you bind on earth, bound will it remain in heaven, et cetera.'

'Yes, Father.'

'Now confess all the sins you have committed in your life.'

'All of them, Father?'

'All those you remember, anyway.'

'Yes, Father.'

The Minister tried to recall his childhood, but the only thing that came to mind was his student years at Alcalá. In no sort of order his memories came tumbling out: light-hearted games, whoring expeditions, student rags, injustices ... Father Villaescusa kept his face entirely expressionless, with his eyes fixed on the female figure that waited contritely on the presbytery steps. Then the Minister gave a rapid summary of his life at court. He omitted mention of the intrigues that had helped him into the position of Chief Minister because he didn't think they were sinful, but the friar questioned him on that score and he had to confess them. The most pressing series of questions and the most inquisitive interventions from the confessor came when the Minister began to tell of his married life, or rather earlier, of the moment at which he had first met the woman who was to be his wife, and had desired her. There came a point at which he said: 'I don't recall anything else.'

But the confessor pressed him further. What a lot of things this tireless inquisitor knew or was able to conjure up in his imagination!

'But is that a sin, Father?'

'Everything that a man who is not in a state of Grace with God does, even his own breathing, is.'

When the penitent said 'No' for the third time, the confessor took over and told him that his sins were so numerous that a whole lifetime of penance would not suffice for them to be wiped away. He should fear not only the torments of hell, but also hell in this life, in the form of moral and even physical suffering brought on by a bad conscience that had not repented. However, he, in the name of the Church, pardoned all his sins, but on condition that he did this, that, and especially the other. 'The other' was that he should renounce all sensual pleasure for the rest of his life, maintaining till his dying day a chaste and exemplary marriage. That being so, *Ego te absolvo ab peccatis tuis. In nomine Patris* . . .

The Minister stayed kneeling in silence for as long as seemed proper. Then he rose, bowed to the altar, and made his way back to the presbytery where his wife was waiting on her knees. When she heard him approach she stood up and went off to make her confession, covering her face with her veil. The Minister tried his best to reflect on those of his sins which had been pardoned on such harsh conditions, but he began to think about his wife as she recalled for her confessor all the details of her life as a girl and as a married woman, holding nothing back. As she concluded and believed she had completely unburdened herself, the friar's thin voice drilled its way into her conscience, rummaged about in it, brought to light the tiny forgotten details, and also all those things for which she had never blamed herself, but which now turned out to be blameworthy. Then it was the description of hell in this world and the next, the loss of peace of mind, the untrusting relationship with her husband up to the moment one of them died . . . The Minister conceived a sudden urge to snatch her away from confession, but he realized that would be a sin too, so he repented of it and thanked God for everything that was happening. When he heard his wife coming back he could tell she was crying, quietly and very privately. The only visible sign was a tear that had fallen on her bodice.

7

This time Father Almeida's carriage stopped at the main gate of the palace. A soldier from the guard came to help him down the step and then stood to attention. Then the Jesuit handed Marfisa out, and they went into the courtyard which was full of

noblemen in court dress and soldiers of the palace guard. There
were greetings from some and curious stares from others. As
they climbed the stairs Marfisa didn't gather up the skirts of her
habit, from fear of exposing to view her buckled shoes and
scarlet hose. Once she stumbled, but managed not to fall by
clutching her companion's arm. Then they began to negotiate
the long passageways.

Colette was waiting behind the door. She opened it and signed
to them to go in in silence. The Jesuit thanked her in French,
Marfisa in Spanish. When the Queen appeared the Jesuit bowed
to her and Marfisa curtsied. The Queen said, 'Please be
upstanding.'

While the Queen adjusted her veil Marfisa had time to inspect
her: she found her pretty of face and well proportioned, though
she judged herself both prettier and better proportioned. She felt
no scorn for her, no envy, and jealousy even less. So they set off,
with the priest in front, then the Queen, and Marfisa at the rear,
along corridors, down staircases, across inner yards. Some may
have wondered who they were, but no one barred their way.
Inside the carriage silence reigned. They stopped not at the
convent but in the nearby square. The soldiers and servants who
were waiting for the Minister and his wife to appear did not
speculate about who they were: what did it matter if a clergyman
and a nun and a lady should go into a convent? The Jesuit
accompanied them to the door. He kissed the Queen's hand and
whispered a time and a place to Marfisa. Now inside the convent
the Queen and Marfisa were alone. There was nobody to be
seen. Without a word Marfisa set off, the Queen following,
through the lower cloister, through the upper cloister, along the
corridors. When they got to Marfisa's cell she said: 'We're here.'
She got her key out and opened the door. The cell was dark and
cool. Still without a word, Marfisa lit the candles in their holders
and the room was filled with half-light.

The Queen had removed her veil and looked expectantly at
Marfisa. Marfisa said: 'My lady, I'm leaving right now. Lock
yourself in, and don't open up until you hear someone knocking

three times with his knuckles. If Your Majesty permits, I'd like
to offer a bit of advice.'

'Is that essential?'

'No, Your Majesty, but it might be helpful.'

'Advice, about what?'

'About how you should act when the King comes.'

The Queen stared at her in silence. Marfisa still had her veil
half on.

'Would you please take your veil off, Sister?'

Marfisa did so, and felt the Queen's closely examining gaze.

'Do you know you're a very lovely woman?'

'That's of no importance, Your Majesty. What matters is
what is to happen here for the good of the King and of the
Queen.'

The Queen went up to her and looked closely into her face.

'Do you know what's going to happen?'

'It's because I know that I ventured to offer some advice.'

The Queen placed her hands on her shoulders. Marfisa bent
her head. The Queen put her hand under Marfisa's chin and
lifted her head.

'Now tell me: who are you?'

'Just a nun, Your Majesty.'

'Were you once married?'

'I have some experience.'

'Tell me what you wanted to say.'

'The King is young, Your Majesty. Young men are in a hurry
and they ruin everything. Calm him down, dare to refuse him,
tenderly. Every "No" should enclose an implicit "Yes". Forget
about time going by. Ah, yes, and here are some blankets in case
you're cold. And in that drawer you'll find half a dozen clean
white cloths. Three ought to be enough, but the saint on the
calendar for today can work miracles.'

The Queen didn't seem to have understood all that well.

'You know the King wants to see me naked?'

'Everybody in the court and in the city knows it. They knew
yesterday. Today the whole country will know.'

'It's utterly shameful!'

'Not at all, Your Majesty. Except for a priest or two, everybody thinks it perfectly normal.'

'What do you think?'

'I've helped you to find a refuge here. This is my cell, but I shan't be coming back to it. I guess they'll turn it into a chapel dedicated to some saint or other.'

The Queen did not reply. She looked around and noticed the bed. Marfisa said: 'It's not worthy of a King and Queen, but that's all there is.'

The Queen stretched her hand out and as Marfisa kissed it she said how grateful she was.

'I hope it all turns out well, Your Majesty. When you next find the King in a cheerful mood, tell him this convent needs a new clock. If he's already waiting out there, I'll keep him occupied for a few moments.'

'Right. But cover your face.'

'We nuns, Your Majesty, are not allowed to speak to a man without keeping our faces covered. Even if it's the King himself.'

'Specially if it's the King himself.'

Marfisa went out. She didn't know it's not proper to turn one's back on royalty, so she did turn her back on the Queen, but the latter didn't notice or pretended not to. The cloister was deserted. Marfisa heard the key turn behind her. She put her ear to the door and waited. The King appeared a few minutes later: his steps sounded as though he was lost, but eventually there he was in the distance, a thin, black, ghostly figure, still unsure which way to go. When he spotted her he straightened up and stepped confidently forward. Marfisa knelt and bent her head. She saw the King's thin hand in front of her, and kissed it.

'Please stand up.'

Now they faced each other: the King, lanky and a bit apprehensive; Marfisa sure of herself, with her head to one side.

'Your Majesty will have to wait a while.'

'Is the Queen here?'

'Yes, but she's only just arrived.'

'Then why must I wait?'

'It's always best, my lord, to give other people time. Things should be taken calmly.'

'What things are you talking about?'

'All sorts of things, Your Majesty. I know what women are like. They like to take their time and have evidence that they're desired. Your Majesty must be tender and careful. Don't be in a hurry. A woman, especially if she's a queen, doesn't give way at the first opportunity. In any case, I make so bold as to say to Your Majesty that once you're inside that cell, there won't be any king or queen, just a man and a woman. Whether they're married or not doesn't come into it. Love knows nothing about laws or sacraments.'

'Why are you telling me all this?'

'Because I've been instructed to tell it you.'

'Did they tell you anything else?'

'Yes, Your Majesty. You should proceed step by step, behave properly, and not get disheartened if the Queen acts a bit prim and proper. It's all part of the ritual.'

'It won't be because they've warned her against me?'

'Surely Your Majesty can judge that by the fact the Queen is waiting for you here?'

'You're right. What do I have to do to get in?'

'You've got to wait a bit, as I was telling you. I also recommended proper behaviour. That haste of yours shows you weren't listening.'

'It's not easy for a king to learn obedience.'

'But what is Your Majesty doing all the time except obey? You obey the Chief Minister, your friends, the laws of the kingdom. You ought to be used to it by now.'

'Yes, you're right again.'

He drew a little apart from Marfisa, went up to the cell door and put his ear to it.

'I can't hear anything.'

'We women, my lord, generally get undressed quietly.'

'You think she'll have got undressed?'

'If she hasn't, why on earth have Your Majesties come to this very uncomfortable place? And wasn't it what Your Majesty wanted?'

'Too many people know that already.'

'Everybody knows. Even I do.'

Marfisa stayed still, with her head bent.

'I'd like to know when you're speaking for yourself and when you're saying what you've been ordered to.'

'It's all bits and pieces mixed up, my lord.'

'May I see your face?'

'The rule forbids it.'

'But I'm the King.'

'Yes, Your Majesty, but the rule is God's rule.'

The King had stretched his hand out towards her veil. He drew it back.

'That's what they say . . .' He listened again at the door. 'Surely she's finished by now, wouldn't you say?'

'In that case, my lord, here's my final piece of advice. Be affectionate, take it slowly, and don't forget that the person in bed with you is a being of flesh and blood. Especially flesh.'

'Who told you all this?'

'A little birdie, Your Majesty.'

Marfisa propelled the King gently towards the door.

'Knock three times, with your knuckles. The door will be opened. Good luck!'

She went off and ran down the cloister, disappearing from view. The King watched her go, and could have sworn that he glimpsed, under her flying skirts, some shoes with buckles and scarlet hose. Once she was out of sight, he knocked at the cell door.

'Come in.'

8

A nearby clock was striking twelve midday. Father Almeida went in through the main gate of the Holy Office building.

When the porter opened up for him, he said: 'His Excellency is expecting you.'

He traversed passages and cloisters with his hat in his hand. The servant who was leading the way stopped: 'It's here.' He opened the door without knocking. Father Almeida found himself in an anteroom in which two servants who were waiting stood up.

'This way, Father, if you'll be so kind.'

He went in. The Inquisitor-General was waiting with his half-empty Etruscan glass of chilled rosé wine before him.

'You're very punctual, Father.'

'Your Excellency told me twelve.'

'And twelve it is. Come with me.'

He led him into an adjoining room where a table had been laid as it might have been for lunch for two monarchs. The glassware glittered and the silver gleamed. Around the socle of Talavera tiles blue monsters raced on a yellow background, and there were dragons with flowery tongues and arboreal tails twirling around each other, endlessly repeated. The Inquisitor indicated a chair for the Jesuit.

'Thank you, Excellency,' and he sat down. The Inquisitor sat down too.

'What weather we've suddenly got landed with!'

'Yes, Excellency. Winter's come quickly.'

'And when does Your Reverence expect to leave?'

'Today rather than tomorrow.'

'You'll find plenty of rain as soon as you cross the Pyrenees.'

'I expect snow as well.'

'And danger?'

'Danger, Excellency, is my companion on this mission.'

'Well, there are places where you'd find a better refuge. Wouldn't you prefer Rome?'

'Rome doesn't attract me. I'll settle for the fog and the dangers of London.'

'There are no fogs here, but dangers there certainly are.'

'I know that.'

The Inquisitor made a sign to the waiting servant. A steaming tureen appeared at once, filled to the brim with fragrant vegetable soup. Each served himself a polite portion.

'You haven't taken much, for the needs of so young a body!'

'I subject my body to strict discipline, but not as much as I should.'

'Do you still perhaps feel some of those prickings of the flesh that torment young clergymen, which give officials such as myself so much trouble?'

'I still have violent urges, Your Excellency, yes – to overturn everything by brute force when I see an injustice.'

'That's bad, believe me. The unmistakable sign that one has reached a proper maturity is a realization that there always will be injustices and misdeeds.'

'But not always the same ones.'

'That's right.'

The Inquisitor started to eat, and the Jesuit did too, quickly and without a further word. After a few minutes the waiter removed the dishes and brought new ones belonging to the same elegantly distinguished service. The Jesuit studied his plate with close attention.

'They're not Portuguese, Father. I know they make lovely china in Portugal, but I inherited this set from an ancestor whose ideas of refinement took a different direction.'

The waiter had returned with the joint of meat. He went up to the Inquisitor, but he signed to him to serve the Jesuit first. Father Almeida helped himself to a reasonable but not excessive portion.

'It's the loin of pork I promised you, Father.'

'It's smells jolly good!'

He waited for his host to serve himself and start to eat. Then he started himself, calmly savouring each mouthful.

'It's pretty good, isn't it?'

'Yes, Your Excellency, it's really splendid. One feels sorry for the Jews who are denied it.'

'Yet, if they've converted . . .'

'But the converted ones, Excellency, feel a certain distaste for it.'

Father Almeida evidently felt no such qualms. The wine was the chilled rosé the Inquisitor was so fond of: he sat drinking it from his Etruscan glass, but the Jesuit's glass was in no way inferior to it, though modern. He certainly wasn't turning up his nose at the quality of the wine.

Then for dessert they brought newly picked oranges and other fruit of the season. Father Almeida chose melon, As they finished, the Inquisitor indicated a place at the folding side-table on which glasses were set for liqueurs and two or three bottles: Chinchón brandy, Andalusian grappa, and a bottle of sweet port. The Inquisitor took port and the Jesuit grappa. As they drank they conversed about this and that, while the Jesuit wished they could finish once and for all with the small-talk and get on with the serious items. They did so as soon as the host, having finished his port, took a folded paper from his inner pocket.

'Take a look at this, Father.'

Father Almeida unfolded it and began to read a lengthy denunciation in which various clergymen, with Father Villaescusa in the lead, demanded that Father Almeida be arrested and subjected to full interrogation by experts, so that his views on Church doctrine could be brought into the open. He finished reading it, folded the paper, and returned it to the Inquisitor.

'What do you say to that, Father?'

'After what happened yesterday, I'm not surprised.'

'I don't know if you too saw that they're also asking for a great auto-da-fé to be held urgently, in which without delay we'd burn all the judaizers, Moors, heretics, and witches we can lay hands on.'

'Yes, that's the second part of the document.'

'And what do you think about that?'

'I'm not in favour of such bonfires.'

'Nor am I. But the people of this country, or at least, of this city, just love the smell of scorched flesh. They may even prefer it to bullfighting.'

'I'm not well acquainted with such people. I'm a subject of the King of Portugal and have lived many years in Brazil. We didn't burn anybody there, and it wouldn't have occurred to anybody that you could burn a fellow-being at the stake.'

'Those are new lands, Father, and a new world is being born there, which may well turn out better than this old one. But the fact remains that those half-dozen distinguished theologians are demanding your arrest and a celebratory bonfire. I'm obliged to arrest you. As for the burning ... that's up to the secular authorities since, as you know, we don't actually do any burning.'

'Yes, I know. The theologians have invented an irreproachable subterfuge. They don't burn anybody, it's the State's execution-ers who do it.'

'Does that seem wrong to you?'

'I fully realize, as Your Excellency does, who those truly responsible are. What does it matter who sets fire to the pyre?'

'You find it unjust?'

'I find it criminal.'

'You must be aware that justice and criminality obey human criteria.'

The Jesuit did not answer. The Inquisitor poured himself half a glass of port, took a sip and rolled it round his mouth. He thought he could hear the Jesuit murmuring, 'Seek ye first the Kingdom of God, and His Righteousness, and all these things shall be added unto you.' He set down his glass and looked hard at his guest.

'You should be aware, Father, because it's important for you, that what we're looking for here is precisely that which shall be added.'

'I'm beginning to understand that.'

There was a pause. The Jesuit was afraid that after it the Inquisitor would send him away, perhaps on the pretext of taking a nap, which would be an excellent way of indicating what was being added at that moment. So he hastened to say: 'Before I leave, and in case Your Excellency has no opportunity in the future to hear me again, I should like to make a confession to you.'

'Certainly, Father, but remember that I shan't be making an

order for your arrest till three o'clock. Things tend to go slowly, and I don't think my men will get to the Society of Jesus's house much before four. The Calle de Toledo is quite a way off.'

'That is so, and I'm grateful for the warning, but all the same I must tell you that right now our lords the King and Queen are together at a certain place in the city, and nobody's spying on them. I hope that at last they've been able to see each other naked.'

'And where are these so much desired nuptials taking place?'

'In a cell in the San Plácido convent.'

The Inquisitor shook his head.

'That cousin of mine is always getting herself into trouble. One fine day I shall just have to send her an official visitation.'

'The King and Queen have been able to get together thanks to a plot personally hatched by Count de la Peña Andrada and myself, helped by a woman called Marfisa, about whom Your Excellency will already have details.'

'I should jolly well say I do! There's a warrant of arrest already out against her, awful rascal that she is! But I don't think the matter will go further than that.'

'She was forewarned about her impending arrest in time, thank God, and thanks also to the kindness of certain Christian souls.'

'And how did it happen, Father, that you got mixed up in this affair? I mean mixed up in the practical outcome, not in the merely academic debate we had yesterday.'

'I've come to think, Excellency, that God brought me here solely for that purpose.'

'So you believe God is concerned about whether the King and Queen copulate naked or in their nightdresses?'

The Jesuit stared at him perplexed. Then he boldly asked him: 'Excellency: do you believe in God?'

The Inquisitor-General smiled gently, but the smile was transformed into a sad grimace.

'A lot of books have been written about God, but they all end up with one word: either "Yes", or "No".'

9

Father Villaescusa, in full canonicals, advanced down the central aisle of the church, preceded by three altar-boys with cross raised and tall candles. The priest walked round the penitent pair still kneeling before the presbytery, went up the steps and stood in silence with his back to the couple. The Chief Minister touched his wife on the shoulder. They both stood up and with the candles going on before walked to the stairway that led into the choir. The altar-boys stayed back as the couple began to climb a narrow stone staircase which turned spiralling in on itself. On one of the bends the Minister's wife said: 'I'm getting dizzy. I'm afraid of falling.'

'Just a few steps more. We're nearly there.'

The lady made an effort and pushed her trembling body upward. The Minister was close behind, ready to catch her in his arms if she should fall.

Up in the choir the nuns of the convent had arranged themselves in a wide oval, looking outward. The Mother Superior presided on her special chair. The Minister bowed and his wife curtsied to her. The nuns nearest to them drew back a little so that Lady Barbara could enter through the gap. She did so, and the nuns sang Mass, responding with one well-trained voice to the Latin phrases sung in his scratchy sharp tones from the altar by Father Villaescusa. The Minister clutched the choir railing and waited. There was no one in the church except for the officiating priest and the altar-boy helping him. When they finished the *Sanctus*, the oval of nuns parted again and the Minister entered the holy space, after which the nuns again closed it. The bell for the canon sounded and in response the nuns began to sing Psalm 51: 'Have mercy upon me, O God, according to Thy loving kindness . . .' They sang softly and it seemed distantly. The Minister could see his wife lying on a little mattress. She gave him a look full of alarm.

'Be strong!' he whispered, lying down beside her.

The lady asked: 'Surely all this must be sinful?'

'If it is, the blame is not ours.'

With all due modesty she began to roll her skirts up. She was wearing stockings half-way up her thighs, and no drawers. The Minister looked away.

'Against Thee, Thee only, have I sinned, and done this evil in Thy sight . . .'

The bell sounded again in the distance. The nuns were still singing their psalm. The Minister and his wife couldn't see what was happening at the altar, but nobody could observe what they were doing either. His will and hers jointly and powerfully resisted the temptation to feel any pleasure, but the struggle to achieve this kept them both tense, even though their bodies had already joined. The Minister's wife cried 'Kiss me!' The Minister did so and the wall of willpower collapsed at once. The Minister felt pleasure coursing along his veins into his bodily extremities, and he buried his face on his wife's neck. She did not move, but sighed long and contentedly. The sigh – 'Aaaah!' – filled the empty space. It meant nothing to the nuns, but the priest heard it with a satisfied smile.

The nuns sang the *Benedictus*, and the door opened so the Minister could come out. After him it opened again and his wife appeared. She wore a veil now, and had hiccups. She knelt at her husband's side, and he tapped her affectionately on the arm: 'Forget it!' Mass went on. The nuns sang again, and after the priest had given the blessing they filed out in order. Now they were alone in the church, the Minister and his wife.

'There, that's over. Let's go.'

'And was that a sin?' she asked.

'Only the Lord knows.'

They set off down the spiral staircase. 'Keep one hand on the railing, and put the other on my shoulder.'

Eventually they got to the bottom. The lady leant against the wall.

'Wait till I calm down a bit.'

She was still crying, but she felt very happy.

10

The couple appeared at the church door. The escorting arquebusiers and the foot-servants fell into line. There were also two
strangers waiting, covered with the dust of the roads, the plumes
on their hats wilting. The first went up to the Minister and held
out a letter, covered in seals but battered about.

'A dispatch from Flanders, my lord.'

Then the second man came up, his letter in somewhat better
state: 'A dispatch from Cadiz.'

The Minister was unsure which to open first, which of the
two might bear the more terrible news. He thanked the couriers,
and opened the report from Cadiz, which told him that the
whole fleet had got safely into the bay, but four of the escorting
frigates were still battling with the English and were in a
desperate situation. 'Pretty good, then!' The other report told
him that the Spanish forces had won a great victory over the
Protestant rebels. 'Thanks be to God!' Father Villaescusa
emerged from the church, and the Minister held out the dispatches for him to read.

'It's logical, Your Excellency. All yesterday evening the people
marched in procession along the city streets begging for God's
mercy.'

'Observe the dates, Father. The victory was won more than a
week ago, and the fleet got to Cadiz the day before yesterday:
precisely the day the King went out whoring.'

The Capuchin proudly raised his head: 'Time doesn't exist in
the mind of God, Excellency. He gave us the victory in Flanders
and favoured the arrival of the fleet because He knew in advance
about our prayers and the sacrifices of our people. I give thanks
to the Lord and praise the excellent idea of whoever organized
the processions. Now, Excellency, this would he a fine time to
celebrate our triumph with a good auto-da-fé. Eighty or ninety
heretics burning up would be a fitting way of showing our
gratitude to the Lord.'

'But you're aware, Father, that for that festivity we have to take the opinion of the Council of Castile.'

'Bah! A couple of dozen noblemen who had Jewish grandmas or great-grandmas. You can never trust them. Rather take the opinions of a dozen clergymen of untainted lineage, and you'll see they agree with me.'

The Minister was about to reply to this when the King and Queen appeared at the convent door, affectionately arm in arm and wearing big smiles. Everybody knew at once what had happened. Before he went over to greet them formally, the Minister asked the friar: 'You know about all this?'

The friar answered: 'Yes, Excellency. Processions, flagellation, sacrifices, all that worked more powerfully in God's heart than the sinful desires of that couple.'

While he was saying this, the Minister had gone over to the King and Queen. He took his hat off and knelt down.

'Please be upstanding, Count. And put your hat on.'

'Put my hat on?' the Minister repeated as though in a dream.

'Yes. I wish you to be the first to receive some benefit from my happiness. But that doesn't stop me from asking what you're doing here.'

The Minister took the dispatches from his breast pocket.

'My lord, I want you to read these papers before anyone else sees them.'

The King read them calmly and attentively.

'Well!' he cried. 'I'll finally be able to make the Queen a present of a new dress.' He turned to her. 'We've won a victory in Flanders, and the fleet from the Indies has reached Cadiz safely.'

'Thanks be to God!' the Queen exclaimed, and without bothering about the number of people looking on, she gave the King a kiss on his cheek.

The Minister's wife trembled all over. How she'd have loved to be able to kiss her husband, just like that, in public, at the church door! But she didn't dare. Instead, she stepped forward and curtsied to the King and Queen. When he told her to rise she ventured to say: 'Thank you, my lord, for the honour you have bestowed upon my husband.'

'I'll do more for him yet, if things go on as well as they're doing at present.'

In the background Father Villaescusa was hovering, waiting for a chance to intervene. He found it after the King had told the Minister that the arrival of such joyful news deserved to be celebrated with great fêtes for the populace: bullfights and fireworks, that was what they liked best.

'And a good auto-da-fé, Your Majesty, surely that's the best way to give thanks to God?'

'Scorched flesh smells bad, Father, and for some reason the wind always carries the stink towards the palace. I'm not in favour of such things.'

The friar merged again into the background, but his mind began to contrive a method by which he might participate personally in what was being planned, if possible to spoil it.

The Minister returned to the King's side.

'My lord: I don't see the royal coach anywhere. May I offer mine for you to return to the palace?'

'What about you? Will you go home on foot?'

'Why not, Your Majesty? It's not far, and it's a good thing if the people can see those who govern them down at their own level from time to time.'

II

The gossiping groups in the square before San Felipe church were still at it. A nameless gentleman came up at a run: 'Great news! Great news!' he shouted, his cape flying around him like an angel's wings. Everyone gathered round him, and someone advised him to calm down and, if possible, take a drink of something, since his tongue was hanging out like a thirsty dog's. From somewhere there appeared a jug of wine, and the man put it to his mouth and drank deep.

'All right, do tell us, what's happened?'

'I hardly know where to start. But I've seen the King and Queen come out from the San Plácido convent, looking cheerful and contented. Then there's dispatches from Flanders, where we won the battle, and from Cadiz, where the fleet has arrived with its cargo of gold and silver.'

'And could you tell from the King's and Queen's faces whether they'd been sinning?'

'I already said they came out looking cheerful.'

'That means,' said a voice, 'that the abbess of San Plácido acted as procuress for them.'

'What I think,' an oldish man with a Catalan accent chimed in, 'is this: the King and Queen sinned, we won the battle and we've got the gold. The gold business is important, you understand. I know the Genoese bankers had told the Chief Minister they wouldn't advance us a single doubloon more. That's why the situation was so serious. How was the country going to survive without another doubloon or two from the Genoese?'

'But now we'll have to repay them what they sent us earlier, and once again we'll have our backs to the wall.'

'As soon as they've got back what is owed to them, with interest, they'll be lending again.'

'And so it goes on, doesn't it? Living on borrowed money and always worried that if the King and Queen commit a sin, the fleet won't reach harbour.'

'We've just now seen, if the news is true, that there's no connection between the two things.'

'We'll see tomorrow what the priests have to say.'

'The priests can say what they damn well like. The main thing is the gold is here.'

'And that the King and Queen seem to be happy, unless this gentleman was mistaken.'

'Was I going to tell you lies? I didn't hear it from somebody, I saw it myself, and pretty close up as well. They were like a pair of newlyweds.'

'But what was the Chief Minister doing at this time in the San Plácido convent?'

'I couldn't find out anything about that. I expect he went there to give the King the good news.'

'In that case, he knew where the King was.'

'As it's his duty so to know. The King can go where he likes and do what he wants, but the Minister has to know. That's why he's got his informers out.'

A gentleman with the cross of one of the military Orders spoke up: 'Come, gentlemen. The fact is that the King and Queen are happy, that we've won in Flanders, and that the fleet from the Indies got here safely. That's absolutely splendid. Now there'll be festivities so that the people can have a good time, and the Crown can pay its debts.'

There was on the edge of the group a gentleman of unprepossessing appearance – spectacles, a big nose – who had held his peace and listened attentively to all that was said. Now he spoke up: 'Gentlemen, I am appalled at the light-heartedness with which this matter is being discussed. We've won the battle, yes, but how many shall we lose in the future? This year's fleet has got to Cadiz, but will next year's get here? The King and Queen may be happy enough now, but how long will that happiness last? It won't be long before we have cause to be gloomy, and when that happens, we'll ask ourselves in our consciences that question nobody dares to pose: why, if we are defending the true faith, is the Lord not helping us? I strive to understand the world, and I fail, and when that happens, I clutch on to a redhot nail: there are sins, we know not what they may be, for which the Lord is punishing us. Are they sins the King is committing or are they those of the people as a whole? Or could it be that God has simply changed His chosen people? I was born in the reign of Philip the Great. That was a real king for you, and our people then really were a nation, and what times they were.'

He had spoken in a rather booming voice, with a certain solemnity, and a tone appropriate to a funeral. He had the effect of damping all the enthusiasm. People drifted off without a glance at each other or at the speaker. It was lunchtime anyway. Someone muttered he was a wet blanket.

I

Marfisa didn't have to wait long. First the Jesuit arrived, calmly and without baggage; then Count de la Peña Andrada, with Lucretia on his arm, convincingly queenly, so haughty and contented did she look. As soon as they had assembled the carriage drew up, with a coachman dressed in black and two chests on the box. Marfisa recognized them as hers.

'But how did you manage to get them out of my house, that being all sealed up?'

'The front door is sealed, but not the back one. That's the one I used,' said the Count. 'All your possessions are in there – dresses and adornments, and also the savings you had stowed away.'

'More than two hundred ducats!'

'Two hundred and twenty-seven, to be precise.'

Marfisa seemed enormously relieved.

'That's great!'

The Count urged them to get on board. Marfisa sat next to the Count, and Lucretia beside the Jesuit.

'I shouldn't mind knowing where we're heading for.'

'Rome,' said the Count. 'It's the safest place.'

They left the city by the Puerta de Alcalá, where their papers were inspected: the Count spoke briefly to the guard and gave him a bribe. Once they were through the gate the carriage shot off at speed. Lucretia went to sleep, as did Marfisa soon after.

'They've dropped off,' observed the Jesuit.

'I put them to sleep,' the Count replied.

'Shall we be going now?'

'It's the right time.'

At a sign from the Count the carriage stopped. They opened the door and got out. The Jesuit had not till then studied the horses in their shafts. The Count followed his eyes.

'They're not vicious. You can choose any one of them.'

The Jesuit mounted the nearest one, which was black. The Count went over to the chestnut and slapped it.

'Shall we go?'

'Well, I . . .'

'How far are we travelling together?'

'I'm going to London, via Paris.'

'I'm heading for Rome, via Barcelona.'

'So we go together more or less as far as Saragossa.'

They put spurs to the horses and set off. The carriage started off too, following them, but already well behind.

When Marfisa and Lucretia awoke they found they were alone.

'Where have those two gone? I didn't hear them get out.'

'To hell, that's for sure. I thought it a bit steep that they'd come with us.'

'There's just the coachman left.'

Indeed, the darkly dressed coachman was using a long whip on his black horses, first a lash from right to left, the next from left to right, like a robot. The coach went along smoothly, as if the road were made of glass.

'You know, there's something I don't understand.'

'You're lucky if you understand some parts of it, 'cos I don't get it at all.'

'And what's going to become of us?'

'Look, dear, God will decide. My mum taught me that with your legs open you can go to the ends of the earth. And Rome must be a bit closer than that.'

Lucretia thought for a moment, then said in a low but firm voice: 'There's a lot of whores in Rome.'

'Then one more won't make much difference.'

If there was to be competition, the awareness of her own charms and skills caused her to smile: what had been her strengths at the Spanish court were surely going to be useful still in Rome.

'I'm getting hungry,' said Lucretia.

'See what's in that hamper they left there beside you. I can smell food.'

Lucretia investigated the contents. There was a bit of everything, even wine.

'Is there enough to last us the whole journey?'

'How can we tell how long it will last? When the food's all gone, we'll see.'

So they ate. Lucretia nodded off eventually. Marfisa as she drifted off to sleep reflected that in Rome there'd be lots of handsome youths of the sort that are good in bed. Even if they are clergymen or bishops. Then Lucretia woke up.

'I need a pee.'

'Just pick up that cushion where your bottom is. I'm sure you'll find a hole underneath.'

There was. The horses went on at a good speed, and there were no stumbles or bumps in the road.

2

The thing about the wind was that it came and went suddenly, leaving a chill behind. There was a mist too, first just a few wisps here and there, then a dense mass of dark grey fog which settled on the city and filled it like an invading army, streets, squares, passages. It got in through cracks and darkened the interiors of the houses. The oldest inhabitants couldn't remember anything like it. It got up people's noses and seemed to clog their minds. It went on for hours but then, as suddenly as it had come, it vanished, taking away a lot of memories with it. When the wind returned it found the city as if nothing had happened, with everybody in a cheerful mood because there was a proclamation about fireworks to commemorate a victory that didn't matter to a soul. Still, already the mules were traversing the roads of Andalusia loaded down with gold and silver and other immensely valuable objects, and that did matter, because each in his way expected to have a share of it. Father Rivadesella would have liked to talk it all over with the devil, but that evening he didn't show up.

3

The officer commanding the Holy Office's men asked the Chief Inquisitor for an urgent audience. The Inquisitor received him while still feeling drowsy, like a man emerging from an interrupted nap which he planned to resume.

'Is it something serious?'

'That Jesuit, Your Excellency. They don't know him in the Calle de Toledo, and no one knows anything about him. They wonder if was an impostor.'

'Eh? What Jesuit?'

'Father Almeida.'

The Inquisitor gave a great yawn.

'He'll be one of those priests who come and go as they please. I guess that's it. Station your men at all the city gates, though I doubt if anyone'll catch him. He'll be heading off somewhere, but I wonder where?'

The captain agreed, and withdrew. The Inquisitor returned to his armchair and sank into the cushions, but before closing his eyes he smiled, because there opened up a bright patch in his memory as though the clouds were parting. 'I expect he's going out through La Coruña. It's the most logical way.' But just before dropping off he wondered: 'Who is it that's going via La Coruña, and why?'

4

The Chief Minister finished writing in his own hand a dispatch which read as follows: 'To H.E. the Spanish Ambassador to the Holy See. Esteemed friend: there will be coming to Rome by the usual route as courier from the King and special envoy a Capuchin friar, Gaspar de Villaescusa, a man of considerable learning whom you should treat with the greatest respect, lodging him as his rank demands. He bears with him a paper which under no circumstances must reach the Vatican: you will know how to handle this. As for the friar, we shall have no need of him for a long time to come. When he does return here, we trust that his asceticism will have been tempered by his experience of good cuisine and excellent beds. He ought to come back convinced (for example) that rather than burn Jewesses it's better to go to bed with them. All of this, my lord Ambassador, I entrust to your intelligence. Your friend . . .' The letter was signed with the Minister's full name and title.

He read it over, folded it, covered it with seals, and rang the bell. A functionary from his secretarial service came in.

'Find our fastest courier and send him off to Rome, via Valencia, where they'll put a galley at his disposal to get him there as soon as possible. He'll have the status of royal courier, and have his expenses in advance. Tell him to come here and pick up the message.'

After the courier had come and received his orders, the Minister sent for Father Villaescusa. He came at once.

'Father, things being as they are, I think it best for you to undertake the journey to Rome we were talking about, for the purposes we agreed. I'll put a good coach and a mounted guard at your disposal, since we know the roads through the Catalan mountains are not all that safe. You could do the trip in seven or eight days.'

'When should I leave?'

'There's a lot of paperwork, Father. If I speed it up, everything should be ready in three or four days. The proposal has to be accompanied by a letter from the King, and he's pretty busy these days; indeed, he hasn't been seen outside the Queen's rooms. You go to your Franciscan house and get things arranged with your Order, but don't delay longer than you can help. You'll undertake the journey with the rank of Royal Courier

Extraordinary, on generous expenses, since, thanks be to God and to your prayers, the palace coffers aren't empty any more.'

The Capuchin seemed content, and went off bowing and scraping and murmuring promises of speedy action.

'All the same, Excellency, don't forget my advice. What we weren't able to achieve when we proposed it may still be possible after suitable training. Chastity within marriage, Excellency, that's my final word.'

'My wife and I are most grateful to you, Father. Our hopes rest on that.'

When the Capuchin had left, the Minister gave orders about preparations for his journey through the Pyrenees and the south of France, which was the easiest route.

The captain of the guard asked permission to come in. He had a paper in his hand.

'I can't find him, Excellency. In the Calle de San Bernardino there's no mansion, and nobody knows this Count.'

'What Count?' asked the Minister.

'Count de la Peña Andrada.'

'Right. Leave the paper. You may go.'

When the captain had left, the Minister read the warrant for the arrest of a Count he himself couldn't remember. He called his chief secretary and held the paper out to him: 'Do you recall this man?'

'I don't, no.'

'Look in the register of the nobility and see.'

The scrivener went out and soon returned.

'There's no one of that name.'

The Minister shrugged his shoulders.

'You may go.'

Then he asked himself: 'How could I ever have signed that paper?' The fact was that a sort of cloud had descended over recent events, but not quite all of them.

5

The great rooms were full of tailors, serving girls, chamber-maids, court dames, and, mistress of them all, the chief lady-in-waiting, duchess of a confused and barren fief. She was busily occupied but a bit envious too, since nobody had ever offered her a dress like the one they were getting ready for the Queen, all pink and silver, with French lace at the neck and on the sleeves and along some of the seams at the waist. The Queen stood in the middle, motionless as a tailor's dummy, waiting while they took measurements and tried this and that on her. To judge by the materials, the expertise of the tailors and seamstresses, and the trouble it was all causing, there wasn't a queen in all Europe who would be putting a lovelier dress on. Already she was thinking who the painter might be who would portray her in it. She'd already asked the King, but he hadn't made up his mind yet. The King stood there, watching from a window embrasure people come and go, listening to all the voices and receiving the tender looks that the Queen – still a motionless but now rather weary dummy – kept sending him every so often. He seemed a bit distracted, and his gaze sometimes wandered away over the distant holm-oaks towards the horizon: his roving eye seemed to be looking for something. What the King could in fact see with his inner eye was the figure of a nun running away, her skirts flying and letting shoes with buckles and red hose be glimpsed. For reasons he hadn't stopped to explain to himself, for some hours past that image had obsessed him: he'd have loved to know who the nun was and what her face was like. The memory of her voice remained with him, indeed it did, but he couldn't recall anything she had said. The voice was familiar, but from where or when he couldn't say. When they took a break from the fitting session, the Queen came over to him with a big smile.

'We must make a visit to the San Plácido convent, to thank the abbess for the favour she did us and to talk about a certain clock they're in need of.'

The King thought this a good idea, but he still couldn't fathom the reason they'd gone there in the first place.

6

Half a dozen devoted followers had accompanied that clergyman with the hooked nose and disagreeable expression to his house. The followers were admirers who praised his poetry and defended it anywhere people gossiped and in the literary academies, while the lower classes said it was obscure and élitist. The master had called them 'ducks on the dirty dishwater of Castile'.

They bade him goodnight at his door. He went in alone, asked what there was to eat as an afternoon snack. They offered him chocolate in a chipped cup. He drank it in an abstracted sort of way and made for his study. The desk was piled with papers all over the place, a few withered flowers, several pens, and a dagger. Don Luis – such was the hook-nosed cleric's name – felt tired, closed his eyes, and stayed like that for a while, as if in a trance. Then he rummaged among his papers and drew out one on which a few lines of verse had been jotted: '*Con Marfisa en la estacada . . .*' He read them over. He couldn't recall how or when he'd written them, nor who they were about, nor even what reason lay behind them. None the less, there began to form in his mind other lines with which he might complete the ten-line stanza. He found a pen, held it aloft for a moment, and then began to write. It no longer mattered who had provoked the rhyme, or when. Here he had something started which it would be as well to finish, which indeed demanded to be finished. Line by line he got to the end. Then he read it over. There were lots of gentlemen in the court to whom he might dedicate it. He headed the paper with a sort of title:

> *To a gentleman who, being with a lady,*
> *was unable to fulfil his desires*
>
> You made so bold, good sir,
> to try Marfisa in the lists of love,

but charged so limply that your lance
could merely scratch, not pierce
the crack within that shield of hers.
No great surprise! With lance again aloft
you charged, were shamed again,
and could not even weep a tear or two
to leave that shield of hers
bespecked with rust around the edge.

SUGGESTIONS FOR FURTHER READING

A great deal has been written on Torrente in Spanish, English and other languages in the last twenty years. Articles in journals and papers collected in books may be traced through *The Year's Work in Modern Languages* or a similar annual bibliography. So far as is known, the present translation is the first into English of any item of Torrente's work. For English readers, there is the useful survey by Janet Pérez, *Gonzalo Torrente Ballester*, in the Twayne World Authors Series (Boston: Twayne, 1984).

FOREIGN LITERATURE IN TRANSLATION
IN EVERYMAN

A Hero of Our Time
MIKHAIL LERMONTOV
*The Byronic adventures of
a Russian army officer*
£5.99

L'Assommoir
ÉMILE ZOLA
*One of the most successful novels
of the nineteenth century and one
of the most scandalous*
£6.99

Poor Folk and The Gambler
FYODOR DOSTOYEVSKY
*These two short works of doomed
passion are among Dostoyevsky's
quintessential best. Combination
unique to Everyman*
£4.99

Yevgeny Onegin
ALEXANDER PUSHKIN
*Pushkin's novel in verse is Russia's
best-loved literary work. It con-
tains some of the loveliest Russian
poetry ever written*
£5.99

The Three-Cornered Hat
ANTONIO PEDRO DE ALARCÓN
*A rollicking farce and one of
the world's greatest masterpieces
of humour. Available only in
Everyman*
£4.99

Notes from Underground
and A Confession
FYODOR DOSTOYEVSKY *and*
LEV TOLSTOY
*Russia's greatest novelists ruthlessly
tackle the subject of their mid-life
crises. Combination unique to
Everyman*
£4.99

Selected Stories
ANTON CHEKHOV
edited and revised by Donald
Rayfield
*Masterpieces of compression and
precision. Selection unique to
Everyman*
£7.99

Selected Writings
VOLTAIRE
*A comprehensive edition of
Voltaire's best writings. Selection
unique to Everyman*
£6.99

Fontamara
IGNAZIO SILONE
*'A beautifully composed tragedy.
Fontamara is as fresh now, and as
moving, as it must have been when
first published.' London Standard.
Available only in Everyman*
£4.99

All books are available from your local bookshop or direct from:
Littlehampton Book Services Cash Sales, 14 Eldon Way, Lineside Estate,
Littlehampton, West Sussex BN17 7HE (*prices are subject to change*)

To order any of the books, please enclose a cheque (in sterling) made payable to
Littlehampton Book Services, or phone your order through with credit card details (Access,
Visa or Mastercard) on 01903 721596 (24 hour answering service) stating card number
and expiry date. (*Please add £1.25 for package and postage to the total of your order.*)

In the USA, for further information and a complete catalogue call 1-800-526-2778

CLASSIC FICTION
IN EVERYMAN

The Impressions of
Theophrastus Such
GEORGE ELIOT
*An amusing collection of character
sketches, and the only paperback
edition available*
£5.99

Frankenstein
MARY SHELLEY
*A masterpiece of Gothic terror in
its original 1818 version*
£3.99

East Lynne
MRS HENRY WOOD
*A classic tale of melodrama,
murder and mystery*
£7.99

Holiday Romance and
Other Writings for Children
CHARLES DICKENS
*Dickens's works for children,
including 'The Life of Our Lord'
and 'A Child's History of England',
with original illustrations*
£5.99

The Ebb-Tide
R. L. STEVENSON
*A compelling study of ordinary
people in extreme circumstances*
£4.99

The Three Impostors
ARTHUR MACHEN
*The only edition available
of this cult thriller*
£4.99

Mister Johnson
JOYCE CARY
*The only edition available of this
amusing but disturbing twentieth-
century tale*
£5.99

The Jungle Book
RUDYARD KIPLING
*The classic adventures of Mowgli
and his friends*
£3.99

Glenarvon
LADY CAROLINE LAMB
*The only edition available of the
novel which throws light on the
greatest scandal of the early nineteenth century – the infatuation of
Caroline Lamb with Lord Byron*
£6.99

Twenty Thousand Leagues
Under the Sea
JULES VERNE
*Scientific fact combines with
fantasy in this prophetic tale
of underwater adventure*
£4.99

CLASSIC NOVELS
IN EVERYMAN

The Time Machine
H. G. WELLS
One of the books which defined 'science fiction'– a compelling and tragic story of a brilliant and driven scientist
£3.99

Oliver Twist
CHARLES DICKENS
Arguably the best-loved of Dickens's novels. With all the original illustrations
£4.99

Barchester Towers
ANTHONY TROLLOPE
The second of Trollope's Chronicles of Barsetshire, and one of the funniest of all Victorian novels
£4.99

The Heart of Darkness
JOSEPH CONRAD
Conrad's most intense, subtle, compressed, profound and proleptic work
£3.99

Tess of the d'Urbervilles
THOMAS HARDY
The powerful, poetic classic of wronged innocence
£3.99

Wuthering Heights and Poems
EMILY BRONTË
A powerful work of genius–one of the great masterpieces of literature
£3.99

Pride and Prejudice
JANE AUSTEN
Proposals, rejections, infidelities, elopements, happy marriages – Jane Austen's most popular novel
£2.99

North and South
ELIZABETH GASKELL
A novel of hardship, passion and hard-won wisdom amidst the conflicts of the industrial revolution
£4.99

The Newcomes
W. M. THACKERAY
An exposé of Victorian polite society by one of the nineteenth-century's finest novelists
£6.99

Adam Bede
GEORGE ELIOT
A passionate rural drama enacted at the turn of the eighteenth century
£5.99

All books are available from your local bookshop or direct from:
Littlehampton Book Services Cash Sales, 14 Eldon Way, Lineside Estate,
Littlehampton, West Sussex BN17 7HE (*prices are subject to change*)

To order any of the books, please enclose a cheque (in sterling) made payable to
Littlehampton Book Services, or phone your order through with credit card details (Access,
Visa or Mastercard) on 01903 721596 (24 hour answering service) stating card number
and expiry date. (*Please add £1.25 for package and postage to the total of your order.*)

In the USA, for further information and a complete catalogue call 1-800-526-2778

DRAMA
IN EVERYMAN

The Oresteia
AESCHYLUS
*New translation of one of the
greatest Greek dramatic trilogies
which analyses the plays in
performance*
£5.99

**Everyman and Medieval
Miracle Plays**
edited by A. C. Cawley
*A selection of the most popular
medieval plays*
£4.99

Complete Plays and Poems
CHRISTOPHER MARLOWE
*The complete works of this great
Elizabethan in one volume*
£5.99

Restoration Plays
edited by Robert Lawrence
*Five comedies and two tragedies
representing the best of the
Restoration stage*
£7.99

**Female Playwrights of the
Restoration: Five Comedies**
edited by Paddy Lyons
*Rediscovered literary treasures
in a unique selection*
£5.99

**Plays, Prose Writings
and Poems**
OSCAR WILDE
*The full force of Wilde's wit
in one volume*
£4.99

**A Dolls House/The Lady from
the Sea/The Wild Duck**
HENRIK IBSEN
introduced by Fay Weldon
*A popular selection of Ibsen's
major plays*
£4.99

**The Beggar's Opera and
Other Eighteenth-Century Plays**
JOHN GAY et. al.
Including Goldsmith's She Stoops
To Conquer *and Sheridan's* The
School for Scandal, *this is a volume
which reflects the full scope of the
period's theatre*
£6.99

**Female Playwrights of the
Nineteenth Century**
edited by Adrienne Scullion
*The full range of female nineteenth-
century dramatic development*
£6.99